WHISTLE
ME HOME

Barbara Wersba

WHISTLE
ME HOME

Henry Holt and Company
New York

For Julie Fallowfield

agent and friend

Henry Holt and Company, LLC / *Publishers since 1866*
115 West 18th Street / New York, New York 10011

Henry Holt is a registered
trademark of Henry Holt and Company, LLC

Published in Canada by Fitzhenry & Whiteside Ltd.,
195 Allstate Parkway, Markham, Ontario L3R 4T8.

Library of Congress Cataloging-in-Publication Data
Wersba, Barbara.
      Whistle me home / Barbara Wersba.
          p.   cm.
Summary: Seventeen-year-old Noli feels as if she has
found her soul mate when handsome, sensitive TJ moves
to Sag Harbor, but even as their feelings deepen,
individual secrets threaten their relationship.
[1. Homosexuality—Fiction.   2. Alcoholism—Fiction.
3. Love—Fiction.]   I. Title.
PZ7.W473Wh   1997   [Fic]—dc20   96-25573

ISBN 0-8050-4850-2

First Edition—1997
Designed by Victoria Hartman
Printed in the United States of America
on acid-free paper. ∞

10   9   8   7   6   5   4   3

WHISTLE
ME HOME

1

TJ Baker is coming down the street towards her, wearing ragged blue jeans, boots, and a white T-shirt—and his face is the face of an angel in a painting Noli saw once in a museum. It might have been the Metropolitan. TJ has a tan, from surfing all summer off the beach at Bridge-hampton, and his curly brown hair is long—almost to his shoulders. He looks so good that Noli begins to cry—she hasn't seen him for a long time—and she steps into the doorway of a barber shop so TJ won't see her. A few steps behind TJ is his friend Walker, who is rolling a cigarette. Walker is tan too, from a summer at the beach, and his blond hair has turned white from the sun.

They look beautiful together. Not handsome, but beautiful. And as they pass her, Noli turns her back to them, to remain unseen. They stroll by, two boys in torn blue jeans, as she cries onto the back of her left hand.

How long has it been? Five months and two days. They parted in March and now it is early August, and after they broke up they did not phone each other. Most people who break up, Noli thinks, at least phone each other—but between her and TJ there was only silence, a deafening silence that turned her into a zombie. She was always thin, but now she is bony and peculiar looking, and she has been chopping away at her red hair so it sticks up in spikes all over her skull. She looks awful, and knows it, but what does it matter? The one person she loves in the world is gone.

After a few seconds she steps onto the sidewalk and gazes after the boys, who are a block away now. Their stride is identical—long and lazy. And they are the same height. Walker's white hair is shining in the sun.

All this is taking place in a town called Sag Harbor, which is on the east end of Long Island, near the ocean, and which is a part of something called The Hamptons. Except that Sag Harbor is not a Hampton at all, not fashionable or chic enough for the summer people. The summer people, the rich ones, have houses in East Hampton or Southampton, and they drive vintage cars and make a whole lifestyle of going to benefits. Benefits for the local theater, benefits for the hospital, or AIDS, or battered women. They also go to gallery openings, and literary readings given by famous poets in tiny bookstores. In the summer The Hamptons is a pain in the ass, Noli thinks. Only in winter, when the summer people have gone back to New York City, does the East End return to normalcy.

Five months and two days. She can hardly believe it because they were so close. It was more than going steady, it was like finding a soul mate. TJ was the new kid in the junior class at Peterson High, and all the girls fell apart over him. Even some of the teachers fell apart over him—he was so beautiful. But the minute he and Noli met, in English III, he chose her as his special friend and asked her to go out with him. That first weekend they went to the health-food restaurant and then to an old film with Humphrey Bogart in it. And all through the film he kept glancing at her and giving her that funny little grin that came over his face whenever he was happy.

Noli's real name is Noelle, because she was born on Christmas Day, but during her childhood it got shortened to Noel, and then it became Noli. "It's a perfect name for you," TJ said. "I bet there's nobody on Long Island with that name." Well, Noli had thought, there probably isn't. But TJ was a good name too. It stood for Thomas Jerome.

TJ's family had moved to Sag Harbor because his father was a writer, and the village was a mecca for literary people. A lot of writers lived there, actually, and the fact that TJ's father had published three best-sellers impressed the hell out of Noli, though she tried not to show it. Her own father was a real estate broker, with offices in Sag Harbor and East Hampton, and he was not an imaginative person at all. Noli's house was in a middle-class development called Baywoods, whereas TJ's family had bought a gorgeous old Victorian on upper Main Street. And his mother was interesting too. She painted in watercolors.

They were both only children, Noli and TJ, and they were crazy about old films, and vegetarian pizza, and neither of them smoked dope anymore. Noli had a little problem with alcohol, but she tried hard not to drink around TJ. They would spend hours reading aloud to each other from *The Way of the Wizard*, or from Gerard Manley Hopkins—

whom TJ had a thing about. His poems were universal, TJ said. Cosmic.

And so it is early August and Noli is standing on the street, crying. TJ and Walker have gone, and there is only the sun beating down on her red hair, and her loneliness, and her grief. Because she is young, she thinks this grief will last forever and she will never be in love again. And maybe it's true.

2

Now we go back to September of the previous year. All the summer people are gone and school is starting. Junior year, Noli thinks, is going to be more interesting than sophomore year—because the courses are better and there are these good electives like "The History of Film." Noli is taking five courses and it's enough. And she is growing her hair a little, because Tracy recommended it. Tracy and she have been friends since kindergarten and they tell each other everything. What's more, they tell each other the truth. No nonsense about making out with dozens of boys in the backseat of cars, or on the beach at night. They are both virgins and admit it.

Tracy and her mom get along pretty well, but Noli and *her* mother have been enemies for years. Noli even dreamed once that she murdered her mother, which frightened her, because she would never harm her—but God, do they fight. They fight about everything, but mostly about Noli's appearance, which is pure tomboy. Her mother thought she would grow out of this phase, but she hasn't—so she wears jeans and hiking boots and baseball caps put on backwards. Once when her mother was out shopping, Noli made a bonfire in the backyard and burned all of her own dresses, and the nightgown she had gotten at Christmas, and two dainty bras. She has never needed a bra anyway, because she is flat-chested.

Noli thinks it is this ongoing war with her mother that started the drinking. The rage she feels at her mother is so strong, and so dangerous, she uses alcohol to suppress it. She keeps a bottle of vodka hidden in her closet, and sometimes raids the family liquor cabinet. . . . Noli sees nothing wrong with alcohol or grass, but TJ is into this new thing of no drugs or stimulants, and vegetarian food. Which is why she became a vegetarian and started eating at The Purple Grape, the health-food restaurant.

Anyway, it is the first day of their junior year, and things are a little chaotic—with everyone trying to figure out their schedules and where the classrooms are in the new wing of the building—when Tracy corners Noli in the hallway on the second floor and says, "I have just seen the most beautiful boy in the world. He's new and his name is TJ. Everyone's falling apart."

Noli gives Tracy a cool look. "You say that all the time. You'd say that about King Kong if he was a junior."

Tracy runs a hand through her blond hair. "Wrong. This one is a Greek god. Tall, skinny, and gorgeous. Cold blue eyes. A tiny little ass."

"God, you're vulgar."

"I can't help it. I would strip for him. I would let him have me."

"You've been reading too many women's magazines."

"I don't care, Noli. He is to die for."

As it turns out, Tracy, Noli, and TJ are all in the same English class. As soon as everyone has taken seats, Tracy nudges Noli and points out TJ, who is sitting a few rows in front of them. A shiver goes down Noli's spine, because her friend is right. The boy is beautiful—with the face of an angel and the body of an athlete. His thick curly hair is longer than any boy's in the room. And he is wearing an earring.

Noli contemplates the small, gold loop earring. She has seen guys in the city wearing just one earring, very macho guys, but the fad hasn't hit the East End yet. She decides she likes it. It has a kind of pirate look.

Their English teacher this year is Mr. Cameron—shy, pale, and humorless. He has been working on a Ph.D. thesis for years and years. People think he is gay, but Noli thinks he is simply washed-out and sexless. He is, however, a very cultivated person. "What did you people read over the summer?" he is asking the class—only to be met by a huge silence. Someone laughs out loud. Then someone else says, "Gee. Who *read*?"

"Now come on," says Mr. Cameron, "didn't anyone read over the summer? Or was it all surfing and rock concerts?"

Somebody's hand shoots up. A boy's. "I read twenty issues of *Penthouse*. My father hides them in the basement."

"Terrific," says Cameron. "Anyone else? Don't all speak at once."

Suddenly, TJ's hand goes up in the air. "Yes, Thomas?" says Cameron.

TJ smiles a little shyly. "People call me TJ."

"All right," says Cameron, "TJ it is. What did you read over the summer? Anything that could remotely be called a book?"

"I read a biography of Gerard Manley Hopkins," TJ replies.

Cameron looks stunned.

"I never heard of Gerard Manley Hopkins," says a boy whose name Noli doesn't know.

"Well, that's your loss," says Cameron. "Hopkins was a great poet."

"When did he write?" a girl named Liza asks.

"In the mid-eighteen-sixties," Cameron replies. "He was a priest."

Everyone groans.

Cameron reaches onto the shelf behind him and brings down an anthology of English poetry. "TJ," he says, "read us some Hopkins."

TJ's face reddens a little, but he mumbles something like, "All right," and then he turns the pages until he finds a poem. As he begins to read, his voice gains strength until it is filling the room—like an actor's.

> *Elected silence, sing to me*
> *And beat upon my whorléd ear,*
> *Pipe me to pastures still and be*
> *The music that I care to hear.*
>
> *Shape nothing, lips, be lovely-dumb*
> *It is the shut, the curfew sent*

From there where all surrenders come
Which only makes you eloquent.

It is at this precise moment that Noli Brown falls in love with TJ Baker. "Falling" is the right word—because she feels like she is tumbling through space and may never land. She feels sick, lightheaded, dizzy, and she is sinking like an elevator into depths she has never known before. The idea that *anyone*—and especially somebody new—could get up in class and read the work of a nineteenth-century priest . . . this idea is dizzying to her. Amazingly, nobody laughs. They just sit there.

"He was famous for something called sprung rhythm," TJ says quietly. "Hopkins, I mean."

"I know that," says Mr. Cameron with awe in his voice. "I know."

3

The bell rings, English III is over, and people rush out the door. It is lunch period, and while some kids will go to the school cafeteria, most of them will head for Luckey's Market where you can take out heros and Cokes and potato chips. There are benches along the sidewalk near Luckey's where people eat lunch and smoke. Everyone departs the minute the bell rings. Everyone except TJ and Noli.

They stand there looking at each other in the empty class-room, and each of them wants to say something, but no words come to mind. TJ is smiling at Noli in a friendly way, like he wants to meet her, but she is too overwhelmed by his looks and the poem he has just recited. Finally, she says, "You read that stuff like an actor. Like Hugh Grant or something."

He grins at her. "I've done a bit of acting. In the city."

"No kidding?"

"I was in an off-Broadway play once. When I was younger."

"Wow. Are you going to be an actor?"

"I don't know what I'm going to be," he says.

Noli pulls herself together and sticks out her hand. "My name is Noli Brown."

"TJ Baker."

They shake hands and gaze at each other.

"I love your hair," says TJ.

Noli laughs. "I cut it myself. My best friend, Tracy, says I look like I've been through a food processor."

"I think it's brilliant."

"*Your* hair is cool," she says shyly. "And I like your earring."

"You want to have lunch with me or something?" TJ asks. "Where do people go?"

"Luckey's. It's over on Madison Street."

Which is how it all began—two new friends sitting on a bench in front of Luckey's Market at eleven-thirty in the morning on the first day of school. Noli is aware that around a hundred people—well, maybe only twenty—are staring at her and TJ having lunch together. Tracy in particular is staring.

Noli and TJ team up again after school and take a walk through Oakdale Cemetery—a place that has graves going back for two hundred years. TJ reads some of the epitaphs aloud, saying words like "Darling we love thee" and "Safely in Heaven" and "Tossed by the sea" and all of a sudden there are tears in his eyes. Noli is startled by this. "What's wrong?" she asks.

He sits down on a stone bench. "It's so . . . loving to put words like that on gravestones. It blows me away."

Noli sits next to him, aware of how quiet the cemetery is.

She has taken shortcuts through it all of her life without really looking at it, or feeling its atmosphere. Now she feels the stillness, and the peace, and she also feels summer dying in the golden air. The air is burnished with summer, but there is a cool breeze coming from the harbor. Autumn in Sag Harbor passes quickly, she thinks. Then the gray days begin.

As though reading her mind, TJ says, "What's it like here in winter?"

She sighs. "It's good—in the sense that all the tourists and summer people have gone. But the whole winter is like, well, *gray*. Entire days of grayness."

"That's beautiful," says TJ.

She cannot get over how sensitive he is, a kind of sensitivity that blends with his maleness. She does not even understand it—this combination of angel looks and athletic body. She feels like she is swimming in the beauty of his curly hair and golden skin. But his smell is the smell of a boy, just a little sweaty, and she likes that. She wonders if there is a word for the combination of things he is—a word that would bring rich brown curls, a single earring, and a sweaty smell all together.

She opens her book bag and brings out a tiny bottle of vodka. "Want a drink?" she asks. "I always take a nip before I go home."

He looks surprised. "Why?"

"To keep me from killing my mother. Verbally, I mean. We fight a lot."

She takes a swig of the vodka, but he says no when she

offers it to him. "I don't drink anymore," he says. "Or do drugs or anything. I stopped."

"Oh," she says. "Right."

"What's your mother got against you?"

"My looks," Noli says bitterly. "My fucking looks."

TJ smiles. "I think your looks are wonderful. You are like a *gamin*."

"What does *gamin* mean?"

"Street urchin."

"Jesus. Who wants to be a street urchin?"

"OK, let's just say tomboy. Beautiful tomboy."

She bristles at the word. "I am what I am. OK?"

"Why are you so defensive?" he asks.

"Who says I'm defensive?"

"Me."

"Well, I have a hard time at home," she says. "My mom is on my back every minute. To be more feminine, to dress differently. I had a motorbike last year that my uncle gave me for Christmas, but I had a little accident with it, on Route 114, and they took it away. I really loved that bike. But whatever I love, they take it away. Even my dog."

TJ grabs her hand and kisses it. It is an amazing thing to do.

There are now tears in *her* eyes. "Everything I like, everything I do—somehow it's wrong. I can't do anything to please them. I'm just all wrong."

"Not to me," he says.

She is so moved by this that she needs to make a joke of some kind—to lighten the atmosphere. "Listen," she says,

"I read something funny in a magazine the other day, while I was at the dentist's. What I read was this: 'The light at the end of the tunnel is the light of the oncoming train.' "

TJ doesn't laugh. She had hoped to break him up, but he doesn't laugh at all. "If that were true," he says, "I'd kill myself now. Instead of waiting for life to do it."

4

They walk back to town in silence, as the golden light fades and scatters into violet. She cannot get over what he has said, those words about killing himself now instead of waiting for life to do it—but she is afraid to ask him what he means, because the answer might be too sad. They pass the town pond where every Christmas a little lighted tree floats on a raft, and then they pass George's Bookstore where people read their poetry aloud. They pass the Whaling Museum, and she realizes they must have passed TJ's house long ago—he lives on upper Main Street. Then she realizes he is going to walk her home—a lovely, old-fashioned thing to do—that he is going to walk her all the way down to Baywoods.

They pass the movie theater and the Cooper Hotel. They come to the windmill at the foot of Main Street. "Let's go out on the Wharf," TJ says, "just for a moment. And watch the sunset."

The Wharf is empty at this time of year. All the tourist shops have closed and The Anchor—where you can take out fish and chips or cooked lobsters—is only open on weekends now. Most of the big yachts have gone too, back to Florida or wherever they came from, and sea gulls perch on the railings with a blank expression in their eyes. Across the water, Shelter Island glows like a jewel.

Noli and TJ sit on a railing and look out at the harbor, at the few boats still anchored there, and at the North Haven bridge, which is large and ugly but somehow impressive. They watch three swans fly overhead, their wings making a humming sound. They watch the sun begin to sink behind the bridge—a misty orange globe.

She has run out of things to say, and there is a tight feeling in her heart, a kind of anxiety she cannot explain. In one way she feels she has known him forever—but in another way she is on edge, wanting to please him, to say the right things, to seem interesting. She wonders if she does look like a *gamin*, and how he can possibly find that attractive. She wonders how many girls he has made love to.

"Was Gerard Manley Hopkins really a priest?" she asks, regretting the question at once.

But TJ nods eagerly. "Yes, he was, a celibate priest. And he was so religious he would walk with his eyes to the ground."

"How come?"

"So he wouldn't be dazzled by the beauty of the world," TJ says. "So that nothing would ever seduce him."

Noli is floored by this. "That sounds terrible."

"Oh, no. It helped him write his poetry. It cleared everything else out of the way."

It occurs to Noli that maybe TJ wants to be a priest too—
and this thought dismays her. He hasn't said he is Catholic,
but you never know. Maybe he wants to be free of worldly
things, like Gerard Manley Hopkins, and not have to suffer
over sex like everyone else. She herself has suffered over
sex—and she is both attracted and repelled by the act.

"Do you know any Hopkins by heart?" she asks.

"Sure," he says.

"Would you recite some for me?"

TJ stares at the globe of the sun—which has sunk below
the bridge—and after a moment he says, "Here's one I like
a lot.

> *I have desired to go*
> *Where springs not fail,*
> *To fields where flies no sharp and sided hail*
> *And a few lilies blow.*
>
> *And I have asked to be*
> *Where no storms come,*
> *Where the green swell is in the havens dumb,*
> *And out of the swing of the sea.*

She does not ask him what the poem means. It is enough
to hear his voice reciting it—enough to be sitting next to
him on a railing while swans fly by. It is enough to be with
this new person at sunset-time, in the month of September, knowing they are both seventeen and their lives are
just beginning. She thinks of lying next to his hard,

brown, naked body—with its boy smell—and realizes that his nakedness, if she ever does experience it, will not frighten her.

"It's getting late," he says. "I'll walk you home."

On the way to her house—past all the small-town things like the 7-Eleven store and the post office and the Xerox place—he begins to whistle, and his whistling is lovely and very pure. He whistles better than any boy she has ever heard, and though she wants to ask him the name of the tune, she cannot. Her entire past has gathered into one large lump in her throat, and she cannot ask him anything. What she wants to do is swallow the lump—the lump of the past—and walk with TJ into the future.

5

When Noli gets home, her mother is in the kitchen cooking dinner and her father is still at the office. Noli slips up the stairs because she wants to be alone and think about TJ. He has invited her for dinner and a movie on Friday night, and as she lies down on her bed she says a quick prayer—the kind she uses for emergencies. Dear God, she says to herself, I do not deserve this person, but please let me have him anyway. If you let me have him I will cut down on my drinking and try to get along with my mother. I will not shoplift anymore.

Noli's room is a mess—with clothes and books and magazines all over the place—and on top of her bureau there is a little shrine to Alice, her dog who was put to sleep six months ago. There is a photo of Alice, a candle, and her favorite squeaky toy. Alice's leash is curled neatly there too, with the metal ID tag that was attached to her collar. Alice was the creature Noli loved best in the world, but she had cancer, and one day when Noli was at school her mother drove Alice to the vet and had her put to sleep—because, in her words, Noli was evading the issue. So along with everything else, Noli's mother is a murderer.

Noli turns on the radio to some soft jazz and lies back on the bed. And mingled with thoughts of TJ there is the grief over Alice, who was a small black poodle. She was five years old when she died, and if it hadn't been for the cancer she could have lived to be at least twelve. The vet had said so when Noli phoned him.

Without knocking, Noli's mother comes into the room. The first thing she does is to stare at the chaos. And the second thing she does is to look at Noli with distaste. Not disapproval—distaste. "Dinner's almost ready," she says. "Your father has to stay at the office for another hour, so it's just you and me."

"Right," says Noli.

"So will you please wash up?" says her mother.

"Why? I'm not dirty."

It is the kind of remark that drives her mother crazy, and she knows it. Then she remembers her promise to God, to try and get along with her mother so God will let her have TJ. "OK," she says. "I'll wash."

"And put on a clean shirt."

"OK."

Her mother lingers in the doorway. "I want you to work on this room after dinner. It's a pigsty."

Noli knows her mother wants to fight—that only fighting will release the terrible tension inside her—but she is not going to give in. Instead, she will wash up before dinner, and put on a clean shirt, and tidy her room. Any other parent in America would have asked about the first day of school—and how it went—but Sally Brown is too self-involved for this. All she cares about is neatness, cleanliness, and order. No one knows why.

When her mother leaves the room, Noli goes down the hall to the bathroom, to "wash up." She is determined not to fight with Sally because of her promise to God—and also because their last fight, a week ago, was dangerous. They had been arguing about Noli's appearance when Noli's mother screamed, "When are you ever going to wear a dress? *When?*" and Noli had replied, "To your funeral."

Her mother had slapped her—hard across the face—and Noli had walked out the door and stayed away for the entire evening. She had gone to the movies and sat through the film twice, returning at eleven-thirty that night, and she and her mother had gone for two days without speaking. Her father, whose name is Harold, had tried to mediate between them, but it was no good. The words, "To your funeral," could not be erased.

Noli's mother is red-haired and pretty, and wanted to be an interior decorator when she was young. She had taken courses in this subject at the community college and had done well. But marriage and motherhood had spoiled her dream and left very little in its place. It's as though she has never heard of Women's Lib, Noli thinks—as though her idea of being a woman is being a maid. Cooking, cleaning, dusting. The endless laundry.

Noli knows her parents do not have a good marriage and that each of them is lonely. And on her better days she knows her mother loves her. But she and her parents are estranged. This estrangement comes from many things, but mostly it comes from the fact that the three of them never communicate. Frequent fights erupt in the household, but no one ever *talks*.

Noli and her mother eat dinner in silence in the dining room which has flowered wallpaper and a mahogany sideboard. On the sideboard stands a silver tea set, which her mother is always polishing, and pictures of relatives in silver frames. Noli hates the way her mother has furnished this house, but there is nothing she can do about it. The house seems like a bad imitation of pictures in those magazines women are always subscribing to. *House Beautiful. Architectural Digest.*

After dinner, Noli puts the dishes in the dishwasher and goes to her room. She picks up the clothes that are scattered everywhere and hangs them in the closet. She piles up the magazines. She puts books into the bookcase and stacks the CDs near the CD player. She even finds an old dustcloth and dusts the furniture. Then her phone—the one she got for her last birthday—rings.

"Noli?" says a male voice. "It's me."

She feels her heart skip a beat. "TJ?"

"None other. How are you?"

"Fine," she says. "How did you get my number?"

"It's in the phone book."

"Oh. Right."

"I wanted to say good night to you."

"Thank you," she says softly.

"What time do you usually go to sleep?"

"I don't know, around ten or eleven. I like to fall asleep watching TV."

"There's an old Ingrid Bergman film on channel eight. In just a few minutes."

"I'll watch it," she says.

"Well then, good night," says TJ. "See you tomorrow."

She takes off her clothes, puts on an oversized T-shirt, crawls into bed, and turns on her TV. The film is one she has never seen before, *Notorious,* but she cannot concentrate on it because TJ and his voice are filling her like warm sweet wine. She feels filled and sweetened by him, as though his essence has poured into her. It isn't a sexual thing—though sex is part of it—it is something deeper. The expression "soul mates" comes into her mind. . . . She and TJ are soul mates whom life has brought together at just the right time. If she had gone on with her life for one more month—or even one more week—she might have died.

6

He is playing first-string basketball, and he is Rollerblading down the turnpike like greased lightning. He is windsurfing off the beach, or swimming out into Noyack Bay farther than anyone she has ever seen. His summer tan is still intact and he wears white T-shirts, which set off his brownness, his leanness, and make his curly hair look even richer. He is playing every sport you can think of—and then he is reciting poetry or writing a brilliant essay on Alfred Hitchcock for the film class. TJ Baker is an almost perfect human being, and this fills Noli with awe and apprehension. The more she is aware of his brilliance, the quieter she becomes—lest he find out she is not brilliant at all. They have only known each other three weeks, but already are a couple. Their first date was successful.

It was Friday afternoon, golden, sultry, and for the first time in years Noli tried to fix herself up. She washed and set her hair—sort of—and put on pale pink lipstick. She did of course wear jeans, but added a Mexican shirt and some gold chains around her neck. Instead of sneakers she put on sandals, which hurt, but what the hell. Not wanting her mother to inquire about all this, she stole out of the house at five-thirty, leaving a note: "Gone to the movies with Tracy."

She arrives at The Purple Grape, the health-food restaurant, at exactly six o'clock. TJ is waiting for her on the sidewalk and grins as he sees her coming. "Hey," he says, "you dressed up for me."

She blushes. "Not really. It's just the weekend. You know?"

He nods, takes her hand, and leads her into the restaurant—where they choose a table by the window and order vegetarian pizza with a mixed green salad.

TJ is wearing clean blue jeans with a white cotton pullover. Thin blue stripes. Crew neck. "That's a neat shirt," she says.

"I got it in Provence. You know where that is?"

She shakes her head.

"The South of France. I was in Paris with my dad last summer, so I just took off for a week and went to Provence. I wanted to see the places where van Gogh had painted. It was beautiful."

Noli thinks of her own life, which thus far has been limited to Sag Harbor and a few day trips into the city. "I guess you've done a lot of traveling," she says.

"Not really. Just that one trip to France, and a weekend in London when I was little. My dad publishes all over the world. He makes these quick trips to see publishers and agents."

"Do you get along with them? Your parents."

A guarded look comes over TJ's face. "Oh, sure. I mean, they don't understand me worth a damn, but we get along fine."

All of a sudden Noli is telling him about Alice, and how her mother murdered Alice six months ago. She even takes a snapshot of Alice out of her wallet and shows it to him.

"Sweet," says TJ. "A miniature poodle, right?"

"Yes. And she was only five years old. They put her to sleep without my fucking permission. It was like murder."

"Are you ready for another dog? Is it time?"

"Not yet," she says, as the waitress brings their food. "I'm still too upset."

"I'll get you a new dog someday. When you're ready."

She is so overwhelmed by this she cannot reply. And for the next half hour they eat in silence. Then, just in time for the seven o'clock show, they are at the Sag Harbor movie house, which specializes in old films. Tonight's film is *Beat the Devil.*

TJ has paid for her dinner, and now he pays for her theater ticket. And at the refreshment stand he buys her some caramel popcorn. They choose seats at the back of the comfortable old movie house. It is almost empty.

"The thing I like about this place," says Noli, to make conversation, "is that it's so shabby. It's the shabbiest movie theater on Long Island, but it has . . ."

"Character," says TJ, supplying the right word.

The movie—which has old stars in it like Humphrey Bogart and Jennifer Jones—is very offbeat and Noli is not certain she understands it. What she is thinking about is whether or not TJ will put his hand on her knee or something like that. The last time she went to the movies with a boy, he put his hand on her thigh and tried to feel her up, which disgusted her. She didn't even know this guy very well, and there he was, trying to get a cheap thrill. Which is the thing that has always infuriated her about boys—their unpredictable sexual needs, their hard-ons, their gropings.

TJ doesn't touch her at all. But towards the end of the movie he does take her hand and give it a little squeeze, as though to say, Isn't this a crazy film?

"That was one strange movie," says Noli, as they come out of the theater.

"I love John Huston's films," says TJ. "There's something very sinister about them. Look—would you like to go over to the hotel and have a drink?"

Noli is impressed. The Cooper Hotel is the most elegant place in town. "Sure," she says casually. "Why not?"

They enter the lobby of the old-fashioned hotel—where people can have afternoon tea or play backgammon—and head for the bar. The bar is quiet for a Friday night, and from one of the dining rooms piano music can be heard. "I really love this place," says Noli.

"My folks come here all the time," TJ replies.

He orders Cokes for them, which makes Noli's heart sink a little. Before leaving the house she had had some vodka—because she needed a boost and because vodka, supposedly, leaves no smell. But now it has worn off, and she would really like a vodka and tonic with lime. "I have a phony ID," she says to TJ, "if you want booze."

Then she remembers he doesn't drink anymore. Or smoke dope. "Sorry. I forgot you don't drink."

"I used to drink myself senseless," he says. "But those days are over."

He is talking like a man of forty, with a long past, and this fascinates her. "Were you an alcoholic or something?"

"I don't know. But I sure as hell drank a lot. And I smoked grass every day."

"Do you feel better? Now that you don't indulge?"

TJ grins at her. "I'm waiting to find out."

The bartender—who is a young woman—serves their Cokes and gives TJ a friendly smile. Noli can tell how attractive this person finds TJ, and all of a sudden she feels overwhelmed. Overwhelmed that such a beautiful boy is dating her. In another room the pianist is playing old tunes like "My Funny Valentine," and the tiers of bottles behind the bar glitter in the soft light.

TJ begins to hum along with the music, and soon he is singing the words to "My Funny Valentine." His voice is clear and sweet—like he is—and Noli wonders if there is anything in the world he cannot do. Unlike her, he is not embarrassed about his talents. He takes them naturally, without making a big deal.

After a while he pays the bill and glances at her, and she knows it is time to leave. The female bartender gives TJ another smile, a rather seductive one, but he doesn't notice. Taking Noli's hand, he leads her out onto the street.

They walk down Main Street, and because it is the weekend some of the shop windows are lit up. The gift shop, the art gallery, Carol's Antiques. The shop windows are glowing with amber lights and the sky is dotted with stars.

He is whistling again, the same tune he whistled four days ago—and she wonders what the name of it is. She is wondering dozens of things about TJ because he is turning into a beautiful puzzle. On the day they met she thought she knew him instantly, but now she is not so sure. He holds within himself some dark and brooding places, just like she does, and she knows there are things about his life he will never tell her. Affairs with women, his drinking, his relations with his parents. Something makes her feel that he is totally experienced with women, which is why he's being reticent with *her*. He wants to go slowly and gently, so as not to frighten her, and this thought moves her very much.

They have passed the post office and are heading towards Baywoods, her development. And there are no lights to be seen now, only the inky sky with its scatter of stars. "When's your birthday?" TJ asks. And when she replies, "Christmas, believe it or not," he laughs.

"I think that's wonderful," he says. "Mine's in August."

"You're a Leo?"

"Yes, and it's a complicated sign. Leos have got to be the best at everything, but they're really timid inside. You know?"

"Sure," she says, not knowing at all.

She doesn't let him walk her up the driveway, to the front door, because she doesn't want her parents to see them. The thought of her mother meeting TJ at this particular time is more than she can bear. So they stop just a little short of the house, as she thanks him for the evening. "It was beautiful," she says. "Thank you."

She waits for him to kiss her good night, but he does something more profound. He leans down and kisses her on the forehead, as though he were a parent or guardian. "I love you," he says. And then he walks away.

7

It is October—and for Noli everything has changed. Her entire world has been altered since TJ said "I love you." She holds these words in her mind and she repeats them to herself at night, before falling asleep, trying to imitate TJ's voice as he said them. *I love you* are the three purest words in the English language, Noli thinks. They are like diamonds.

Everything looks better to her now, including her parents. She is trying hard not to fight with her mother, and has gone for a few walks on the beach with her dad. She has TJ to confide in, which has changed everything, but her father has nobody. A few nights ago she stepped out into the backyard, to look at the stars, and found him sitting in a lawn chair smoking. "I'm sitting outdoors because I committed a crime after dinner," he says sheepishly.

"Hey, no kidding," says Noli. "What did you do?"

"I used an ashtray."

She snorts with laughter, because she knows exactly what

he means. Dirty an ashtray, rearrange the pillows on the couch, and her mother goes insane.

"You probably shouldn't smoke anyway," she says to her father. "It's bad for you."

He sighs and looks up at the stars. "I never really saw stars until I moved out here. In the city, you never saw them."

"Yeah. Right."

"I mean, there was always so much pollution in the city."

"I know."

"How's school going?" her father asks. "How's junior year?"

"Better than sophomore year. I'm taking an elective."

"Oh?"

"It's on the history of film and it's neat."

She is longing to tell him about TJ—longing to tell him that for the first time in her life she is in love. She wants to tell him how extraordinary TJ is, and how beautiful, and how his very existence is a miracle. He has come into her life like one of those comets she sometimes sees—streaking fire across the sky.

Instead, she says, "How's the real estate market?" Her voice sounds phony as she says this, but she knows it is his favorite topic.

"The market is excellent," he replies. "I sold a house in North Haven last week. Up at the Point."

"Great."

"If things keep going this way, we can build a pool."

"Where?" she asks.

"At the end of the garden. There's room enough—near the lilac tree."

It is amazing to Noli that she and her father are sitting in the autumn night, with a field of stars above and a sweet smell of flowers coming from the neighbor's garden, and they cannot say anything important to each other. Amazing that two people who are related cannot share a single hope or dream. Her father is a sensitive person, but forever and ever, she feels, he will be talking about the real estate market and she will be telling him the trivia of her life instead of the things that are shaking its foundation—TJ, their relationship, and the fact that she wants to marry him. She knows this is crazy—they are both only seventeen—but she wants to marry TJ before they graduate high school. More important, she wants to sleep with him.

This part of their relationship is very strange because TJ has not yet made love to her. He has held her hand, and kissed her gently on the forehead, and once he put his arms around her and buried his face in her neck—but he has done nothing that could be called making out. She feels this will happen sooner or later, but the waiting is terrible. Tracy, with whom she has discussed the problem, cannot believe TJ hasn't kissed her yet, but Tracy finds TJ more sensitive than other boys ... so maybe it's par for the course.

Noli has to admit that the presence of TJ in her life has dampened her friendship with Tracy, but this was bound to happen. Tracy would never show jealousy over a boyfriend, but she *is* jealous inside, and so they don't phone each other every night the way they used to, and weekends are reserved for TJ. She has still not introduced him to her parents, but she has met his—and they are impressive. The father is a professorial type who wears wrinkled chinos and horn-rimmed glasses, and who writes his books in a tower room in the large Victorian house. And the mother is pretty and well-bred and just a little vague—a sweet woman who paints landscapes and who is always joining committees. She can't say no to anyone, and so she has joined the Ladies' Village Improvement Club, the Library Committee, and a group that works with battered women at the shelter. The mother, whose name is Annabelle, simply shakes her head and says, "It's perfectly awful, but I can't seem to say the word *no*."

TJ's parents are so glad to meet Noli, and so hospitable, that she is almost embarrassed. They know she is TJ's new girlfriend and seem very pleased about it. And their house fills Noli with awe because it is so different from her own. All the furniture is family stuff, beautiful antiques, and there is a real library with leather-bound books, and a "garden room" at the back of the first floor that has windows looking out at the grounds. TJ's room is just as messy as her own, but more interesting. He has put travel posters on the walls and has a tiny piano—a spinet—in one corner. He picked it up at a flea market.

Noli has studied the books on TJ's bookshelves, and thinks they are a key to his character. Books on France and England, all of Tennessee Williams's plays, and lots of poetry. The complete works of Jack London and an old, illustrated volume of Edgar Allan Poe. On TJ's bureau is a photograph of his mother when she was a little girl, and Noli finds this touching. She and TJ have sat in his room for hours, listening to CDs and browsing through books.

On one of these evenings she decides to tell him about a bad thing that happened to her when she was little, because she wants him to know her as deeply as possible. She wants him to know her fears as well as her strengths—because what nobody realizes is that Noli is a frightened person. People think she is cool, laid-back, and confident, but inside she is swimming with fear.

Anyway, one night when she and TJ are lying on the floor of his room, listening to Miles Davis tapes, she says, "TJ? There's something I want to tell you. About me. When I was little."

He gazes at her with his pale blue eyes—eyes that are the color of blue ice—and says, "Sure, Noli. Fire away."

She turns over on her back and stares at the ceiling. "It's something I've never told anyone, so it's hard."

He leans over and kisses her lightly on the cheek. "You can trust me."

"OK," she says fiercely. "When I was around seven, all through the first grade, there was this teenage guy who fooled around with me."

A sad look passes over TJ's face. "I'm so sorry," he says.

"He would get me on my way home from school—and no matter how many times I changed the route, he would catch me. Then he would take me into a vacant lot."

"God," says TJ. "Did you have intercourse?"

"No, no, that never happened. But he would make me . . . touch him and everything. And he would touch me."

"That's horrible!" says TJ. "I *hate* men who do that to little kids. It's traumatic."

"Yeah, that's the word. *Traumatic.* Because he'd have a climax and everything, and I would go home . . ."

"Feeling bad and dirty and soiled. I know. I know."

"But the worst part of it was, well, that a part of me liked it. And then I would be overwhelmed with guilt."

"What made him stop?"

"He got caught doing it to some other kid, even younger than me, and he was arrested. And then his family moved away."

"Poor Noli," says TJ. "Poor little girl."

"What I'm trying to say is . . . it still bothers me. Do you understand?"

"Of course I understand! These things affect us our whole lives, but there has got to come a time when you let go of it. You have to turn it over."

"To whom?" Noli asks.

"God," TJ replies.

She is so surprised by this answer that she doesn't speak for a while. "Well," she says, "I guess I haven't done that yet."

"Being a victim is a cop-out. We can't just go through life being victims."

"I know that," she says meekly.

"So many people act like victims instead of taking responsibility for their lives. Not that I don't understand what happened to you, Noli, because I do."

She feels let down by his response—deflated, somehow—but she tries not to show it. Because TJ is so much stronger than she is she probably shouldn't have mentioned the incident in the first place. And if he is into some spiritual thing like celibacy, the story wouldn't be important to him anyway.... She must wait now—and get to know him better. She has always grabbed at everything in life she wanted, so now is the time to wait. It is a kind of lesson.

8

It is wonderful how many of the same things Noli and TJ like—almost as though they are twins. Not just old films and vegetarian food, but browsing in junk stores, going to flea markets, and riding all the way to Montauk on TJ's motorbike to an R.E.M. concert. They both like to walk the bay beach and collect shells, and TJ has gotten Noli into the habit of going to book sales, where they pick up books for just a quarter or fifty cents. They buy volumes of poetry, old novels, and books on Walt Whitman. They find a beautiful volume of classic short stories for three bucks.

It turns out that TJ has another white cotton shirt with stripes—bought in Provence—and so he gives it to Noli. His pullover has blue stripes and hers has red stripes. They both buy white baseball caps and wear them backwards. Noli's hair is longer now, and she intends to grow it *very* long. Then they will be twins, though she herself will never be beautiful. By now, TJ's beauty is almost legendary. Everyone talks about him and has crushes on him, and two of the girls in Noli's class have even asked him out—which makes her falter inside. Both of these girls are attractive, and Noli fears that one day he will succumb.

She has not yet said "I love you" to TJ because she is waiting for the right moment—the moment when the words will come naturally and not embarrass her. Maybe the night of the Halloween dance. This is Peterson High's first social event of the year and everyone is looking forward to it. Maybe late that night she will be able to say the three precious words.

She has been pondering what their costumes should be—and finally decides they should go to the dance as old movie stars. What's more, it would be sort of hilarious to cross-dress. She could be Humphrey Bogart and he could be Ingrid Bergman. In *Casablanca*. It has become their favorite film and they have rented it from the video store a dozen times. They know all the dialogue, and whenever there is a problem at school—any kind of problem—TJ will say to her, in a low voice, "Round up the usual suspects." It breaks her up.

One golden afternoon, when they are sitting by the town pond watching ducks, Noli decides to discuss the dance. The trees around the pond are glowing with autumn colors—burnished reds and yellows—and the sky is a dizzy blue. It hurts your eyes to look at it. The town is peaceful this afternoon, with kids strolling home from school and a hint of frost in the air. On Halloween night people will put lighted pumpkins on their doorsteps and the little children will go trick-or-treating.

TJ is whistling to himself—that same lonely tune—and his mind seems far away. "Listen," she says tentatively, "I have some thoughts about the dance. About our costumes, I mean."

TJ stops whistling. "So? Fire away."

"What I thought was . . . well, maybe you won't like this idea. But what I thought we might do is cross-dress. You could be Ingrid Bergman and I could be Humphrey Bogart. It would really be funny, you know?"

She is shocked by the look of rage that comes over his face—pure, murderous rage. "No!" he says. "No way! Jesus. What ever gave you such an idea?"

"I don't know, I . . ."

"It's a shitty idea! And I will not do it!"

She is stunned by his language, because he has recently stopped her from using four-letter words. She is not allowed to say fuck or prick or any of the other words she used to say so casually. And here he is, using the same words.

Quickly, TJ regains his composure. "People would think we were crazy if we did that, Noli."

"But it's a costume party. People can be whoever they want."

"Not in this town. It's too conventional."

He walks her home in silence, not even whistling, and her heart is as heavy as lead. Maybe this is the end of their relationship, ending—as so many relationships do—over something stupid and meaningless.

But then TJ stops on the sidewalk. The dark thing that leaped out of him is gone, and he gives her a friendly smile. "I think you should go as Madonna—and I'll go as Sylvester Stallone. In *Rocky*. What do you think?"

"Great," she says quickly. "Very good."

"You're little, like Madonna is, and I could look like Stallone. All I would need is some satin shorts, and you could be in a black slip. Remember that Madonna video we saw on TV? All she wore was a black slip and heels, and a silver cross around her neck?"

Noli remembers the video very well. It was startling because it took place in a cemetery and was highly erotic. A beautiful male corpse opened his own coffin, came to life, and kissed Madonna passionately.

"I'll get you a wig at the Town Shop," TJ is saying. "And I'll shape it for you."

She would do anything to please him now—anything to erase the darkness that has come between them. "I love the whole idea," she says. "It's cool."

That night, however, she has her recurring dream—the one she has been having for years—only TJ is in it this time, which makes it more painful. She is lost in New York City, lost without her wallet or her house keys, and she doesn't know how to get home. She is wandering around the city begging people to help her, but nobody will. All she wants is for someone to help her return to Sag Harbor—away from the noise and the traffic and the skyscrapers—but her pleas fall on deaf ears. She begs a taxi driver to help her, and then a man in a big car. She stops a woman on the street and says she is lost. No one will help her. In fact, they don't even listen.

Then the dream changes to include TJ. *He* is there, somewhere in the city, and if she can only find him everything will be all right. *He* will be the one to carry her home, on the back of his motorbike, and he will soothe her fears—but she cannot locate him. The city is made up of millions of people and somewhere in its depths he is waiting for her, and loving her, but she cannot find him. She wakes up weeping.

For the next few days TJ is absorbed in creating their costumes. He will wear purple satin boxing shorts, high lace-up running shoes, and a sweatband around his forehead. As for Noli, he has brought her a black satin slip, made her a silver cross out of aluminum foil, and has found a good-looking black wig at the Town Shop for only ten dollars. On the night of the dance they hole up in his room and work on their outfits.

Noli is sitting on a stool in front of him while he deals with the wig, snipping it here and there, giving it shape. Then he pulls out a makeup kit he has bought at the drugstore and begins to put eye shadow on her, and lipstick. "It's amazing," he says, "you're really starting to look like her."

He steps back to get a good look. "Cute. And very real. I like it."

"Maybe we'll win a prize," says Noli. "The first prize is two tickets to the new theater on the Wharf. Have you ever been there?"

"No, but I'm curious about it. I've even thought of volunteering as an usher or something. So I could watch rehearsals."

She smiles. "You *should* be in the theater, you know. You'd be great."

"The next Anthony Hopkins?"

"Sure, why not?"

"Because my father would hit the roof."

"Well, what does he want you to be? A doctor, a lawyer, a dentist?"

TJ laughs. "You're close."

"You mean, it's all right for him to be in the arts—but not you? That's hypocritical."

Something dark crosses TJ's face—like a cloud crossing the sun. "It's a boring topic, Noli. Forget it."

Two hours later they are in the gym at Peterson High, dancing to some old tunes the band is playing. People's costumes are very good, and Noli thinks maybe she and TJ won't win a prize after all. Mr. Cameron has come dressed as Napoleon and her Spanish teacher, Mrs. Nordio, is done up as Cleopatra. There are pirates and soldiers, ballet dancers and firemen. People look great.

A lot of kids are staring at Noli and TJ as they dance to the slow music because TJ looks incredibly sexy, and he is dancing close to her. They have never danced together before—and the feeling of his body against hers is wonderful. Also, he dances like a pro. "You look gorgeous," he whispers into her hair. "So do you," she whispers back. "People are staring."

They don't win a prize, but a lot of people come up to them afterwards, saying how great they look, and even Tracy and her date are friendly. As a joke, TJ boxes on the dance floor with a kid named Bobby Fitzgerald, and to Noli's surprise he really seems to know how. There is nothing he cannot do, she thinks. He is perfect.

He walks her home around midnight—both of them

wrapped in warm coats—and Noli realizes she is going to have to introduce him to her parents pretty soon. Her mother knows she is dating someone, and has been harping on it. "If you're seeing a boy, I need to meet him," she has said a number of times. "I can't just let you run wild."

When has she ever run wild? She has never been in trouble—except for that accident with the motorbike—and compared to other kids her behavior is tame. But tonight, as TJ walks her home, she feels excited. Because she knows he is going to make love to her.

When they get to her house, she leads him around to the backyard—and they stand together in the darkness, near the lilac tree. There are no lights coming from the house, which means her parents are asleep, and the night is chilly and clear. "I had such a good time," she says to TJ.

At last his arms are around her, and he is kissing her. The kisses are not what she expects—they are so gentle—but they make her happy because she has been waiting for such a long time.

"I love you," she says in a muffled voice. "I really do."

"I know that," he says gently.

They kiss for a while, but Noli can tell that TJ is not aroused. Instead, he seems to be dreaming a secret dream—dreaming about something hidden from her and much too precious to share. His mouth is sweet and vulnerable, like a child's, and at one point she pulls away and touches his lips with her fingers. In the moonlight he looks like a god.

9

She does not introduce him to her parents until the second week in November, and then she does so with trepidation. She is terrified that her parents will do something awkward and spoil everything. But the night TJ comes to dinner everything works out fine. Her mother has cooked one of her special meals—beef Wellington—and her father is jovial and kind. They do not ask TJ too many questions about himself, which they have done with other boys, and after dinner they go upstairs to the den—leaving Noli and TJ alone in the living room. Noli can tell that her mother has been impressed by TJ, and her heart is soaring.

"They behaved themselves!" she says to TJ. "It's amazing."

She collapses on the couch and kicks off her shoes. "Well, at least that ordeal is over. Now you can come here as often as you want."

For no reason, she begins to giggle. Well, actually, there *is* a reason, because she has had some vodka before TJ arrived. She is certain no one can smell it, but out of the blue TJ says, "I wish you wouldn't drink, Noli. I mean it."

She gazes at him with innocent eyes. "What makes you think I've been drinking?"

"Because I can smell it! You think people can't smell the liquor on your breath, but they can. I'm amazed your mother hasn't caught on."

"I never drink around you, TJ. I know you don't like it."

"But you *are* drinking around me!" he shouts.

Once again, his anger comes as a shock to her. He is gentle most of the time, but somewhere inside him there is rage. Only last week a kid at school, a boy named Eugene, teased TJ about something and TJ went a little crazy. He pushed Eugene up against the lockers and banged the kid's head into them, over and over. A teacher had to separate them—and then TJ was put on report. TJ wouldn't tell Noli what the cause of it was, but Tracy said it was TJ's earring. Eugene had said something derogatory about the earring.

Noli is beginning to realize that TJ is battling demons. There are things inside him that cause him terrible pain, and this knowledge strikes at her heart. By now she knows he is not perfect, but she would love him any way he was. If he was a criminal, she would love him.

The one thing that is bothering her—hurting her, really—is their lovemaking. It is December, and nothing has happened between them except kissing. TJ has never put his hand under her shirt to feel her tiny breasts, and she has never once felt him have a hard-on. He kisses beautifully, but it is not like passion. It is more like tenderness. She wants—so badly now—to lose her virginity with him, to give him this sacred present, but somehow they never get there. All he does is kiss, as though he is living in a dream.

She wonders what the dream is made of. She wonders if she is too innocent for him. She wonders if he is trying to be like Gerard Manley Hopkins. What does he really feel, and how can someone so gentle have such anger inside?

"Why do you like me?" she asks him one night, when they are doing homework together at her house.

He looks up from the book he has been studying. "What a funny question," he says.

"No, it's not, TJ. I'm not even pretty."

Quickly, he grabs her hand. "But you are! Not conventionally pretty, but . . . original."

"But why do you *like* me? I've never understood it."

He thinks for a moment. "Because we are two sides of a single coin."

The answer is too abstract for her, and so once again she retreats into silence. She would like to push the subject further, but she is afraid to lest she make him angry. The irony is that the two of them have had more sex education than any kids in the world. From the time they were little they were taught, in school, about sex and commitment and relationships. And here they are, two people in love who cannot even discuss the subject.

Noli has been trying to become feminine for TJ— growing her hair, using lipstick—but this doesn't seem to interest him. Instead, he has been insisting they dress like twins. So they go to the Town Shop and buy matching corduroy pants and boots and pullovers. They buy caps with visors and long trailing scarves. When TJ has saved some money he intends to buy them both English raincoats.

Frost—and pumpkins on the doorsteps. Leaves in the gutters and a cold wind sweeping from the bay. All the trees are bare and they look like witches, their arms outstretched. Noli doesn't like winter, with its short days and leaden skies, but TJ does so she tries to change. Winter means the town pond will freeze over and people will come with bags of bread and corn for the ducks. Winter means cups of hot chocolate after school, too much homework, and rented videos to watch while the first snowflakes fall. Winter is too many layers of clothes, and a sudden tiredness among the teachers at school. They all start out with energy, but by Christmas they fade.

Sally Brown is showing a lot of curiosity about TJ, and it makes Noli nervous. During the first week in December she actually interrogated Noli about the relationship—and the conversation did not go well at all. Noli was simply lying on her bed one night, reading a book, when her mother came into the room and sat down with a determined air, as though she was about to conduct a scene planned in advance.

"I want to talk to you about something," her mother had said.

"OK," Noli had replied, closing her book.

"Honey, it's about TJ."

"What about him? What's wrong?"

"Nothing is wrong. Your father and I like TJ very much. He's a good-looking boy and very smart. And the family is well-off and everything. We're glad you're dating such a nice boy, but . . ."

"But what?" Noli said angrily. "What's the problem?"

"Honey, it's this way. TJ is a very sophisticated kid, and you're not. Your father and I are afraid that, well . . . that the relationship may go too far."

"I don't know what you're talking about."

"We're afraid TJ may try to take advantage of you," her mother said.

And that is when Noli exploded. "Advantage! What do you mean by *advantage*? TJ is the most moral person I've ever met in my life! He's probably going to become a priest or something."

"Noli . . ."

"What do you think we're doing—having sex? Well, even if we are it's none of your business."

"It is very much my business! I'm responsible for you."

"Oh, no you're not! The only person responsible for me is *me*."

"Noli—there has got to come a time when you and I get along. I can't stand this fighting anymore."

"Oh, sure! Then why do you always start it? You try to pick fights with me every day of my life, and then you turn around and say we've got to get along! What bullshit!"

"Don't use that word to me, Noli. You're a well-bred girl."

"No, I'm not! I'm not well-bred at all. Jesus! You don't even know who I am."

"And do you know who *I* am?" her mother had shouted. "Have you ever once looked at me?"

Her mother had walked out of the room at that point, and Noli had burst into tears. Not because her mother thought she was making out—but because she wasn't making out at all.

It was incredible the way her mother talked about sex— as though it was some kind of social problem. Never anything joyful. Never anything to do with pleasure. It was like her mother hated sex and had only endured it in order to have children. There had been another child born to the Browns when Noli was two years old—a little boy—but he had died at six months. And then Sally learned she couldn't conceive anymore. Her father had explained all this to Noli a couple of years ago. "Your mother hasn't had an easy life," he had said. "You should show some compassion for her." But as far as Noli was concerned, compassion worked both ways.

It is Christmas vacation now, and school is out, and the uppermost thought in Noli's mind is TJ's Christmas present. She has made lists of things she might buy him, but nothing seems good enough. He already has great clothes, dozens of CDs, a motorbike, and that spinet piano he is always fooling around with. He has a telephone in his room, just like she does, and a very expensive watch. Then it comes to her. She will go to the rare bookstore in East Hampton and see if they have any poems by Gerard Manley Hopkins.

The bookstore—which is on Newtown Lane—is small and elegant, and Noli has never been inside. She has only looked in the windows. Today, however, she goes in and shyly asks the clerk if he has anything by Hopkins. He nods, reaches up to a shelf, and brings down a small leather-bound volume. *The Selected Poems of G. M. Hopkins.* It costs fifty dollars, a terrible price, but she writes out a check for that amount. The clerk wraps the book in soft rice paper.

She walks to the corner, where she will wait for the bus back to Sag Harbor. Then she undoes the rice paper and looks at the book. It was published in London in 1920, and it seems very beautiful and rare. She turns the pages at random and finds these words:

> *Let me be to thee as the circling bird,*
> *Or bat with tender and air-crisping wings*
> *That shapes in half-light his departing rings,*
> *From both of whom a changeless note is heard.*

Noli doesn't understand the poem, but maybe a person doesn't have to. Maybe the beauty of the words is enough. A bat with "air-crisping wings" is a wonderful image, she thinks, and one that TJ will appreciate. He is much more literate than she. He reads Shakespeare for the fun of it.

As she stands there, the first snowflakes of winter begin to fall—and suddenly she is filled with joy about Christmas. Christmas has always made her sad because it is combined with her birthday, but now that she has TJ everything is new. She is new, the world is new, and TJ loves her. He has told her so a hundred times.

10

She is wakened on Christmas morning by the ringing of the telephone. It is only seven A.M., and she pulls herself out of a dream to reach for the receiver. "Yes?" she mumbles. "Who is it?"

"Merry Christmas and Happy Birthday!" says TJ. "I have to give you your present right away. It can't wait."

"I'm still asleep."

"Noli, it can't wait! Or maybe it's me who can't wait. Let me come over."

"At seven o'clock?"

"Sure, why not? I'll meet you in your backyard in half an hour."

She laughs. "OK, OK. Listen—Merry Christmas."

"Thirty minutes," he says.

She jumps out of bed and runs to the bathroom. Then she pulls on a pair of jeans and a wool jacket, slips down to the kitchen for a cup of coffee, and examines the wrappings on TJ's present. She has wrapped the book in some very expensive gift paper and tied a sprig of holly on it.

She winds a long scarf around her neck and steps into the backyard. Her parents were out late last night and she doesn't want to wake them. The day is chilly and gray, with an overcast sky, and there is the smell of snow in the air.

She hears TJ's motorbike coming down the street, and then the motor shuts off—as though he has parked a distance from the house. Her heart begins to beat fast as she realizes this is the first holiday they have spent together. On Thanksgiving they both had to be with relatives.

TJ comes into the backyard wearing a tweed coat and a wool seaman's cap. He looks eccentric, but beautiful. And there is an aura of excitement about him, as though he cannot wait to give her his present. It seems to be hidden in his coat—a round lump.

He does not kiss or hug her. He simply stands there, grinning. "Happy Birthday and Merry Christmas," he says.

He reaches into his coat and brings out a puppy—small, black, and curly-haired. "Alice the Second," he says triumphantly.

Noli is so surprised she starts to cry. The puppy is a poodle.

"Hey," says TJ, "it's not supposed to make you cry. It's supposed to make you happy! Here—hold her."

He puts the wriggling puppy into Noli's arms and it licks her face, which makes her cry even harder.

"Darling, don't cry. It's your new Alice. And it's OK with your parents. I checked it out with them."

Noli sinks down on the bench by the lilac tree as the puppy continues to lick her face. Then it pees on her lap and she laughs. "God! How old is she?"

"Eight weeks, a real baby. I got her from a breeder in Southampton."

"Oh, TJ . . ."

"It's *time* you had another dog."

"I'm so touched," she says, burying her face in Alice's fur.

"Put her down, Noli. Let her run around."

Noli puts Alice the Second on the grass and reaches into her jacket for TJ's present. "Mine's not half as nice. But anyway, here it is. Merry Christmas."

TJ undoes the gift paper carefully. "I always save the paper," he explains. His eyes widen. "Oh, how beautiful! The poems of Hopkins."

"It's very old. Published in nineteen twenty."

"How lovely! Where did you get it?"

"That special bookstore in East Hampton."

"I'm crazy about it. It's the nicest present I've ever had."

They sit there smiling at each other as Alice plays on the grass. Then, flake by flake, the snow begins. "Come into the house," Noli says to TJ, "and I'll make us some hot chocolate. Oh, wow! I don't have any dog food."

"Oh, yes you do," says TJ. "I have a bag of Puppy Chow on the back of my motorbike."

The day is enchanted. The day is magical—the way Christmas is supposed to be—and not a single thing goes wrong. Noli and TJ drink hot chocolate in the kitchen, and when her parents come down the stairs they all open presents together. Her parents have bought TJ a cashmere scarf, which surprises Noli, and because it is her eighteenth birthday, as well as Christmas, they have bought her a beautiful opal ring circled with little diamonds. They play Christmas music on the radio and everyone laughs at Alice—who is tearing up the gift wrappings.

TJ has not only brought a bag of Puppy Chow, but a tiny collar and leash. And so, after breakfast with the Browns, he and Noli take Alice for a walk. Alice doesn't know how to behave on a leash and gets tangled in it, so TJ picks her up and carries her. The snow is falling in great white flakes that seem unreal.

"Where shall we go?" TJ asks Noli.

"Would it be strange to walk up to the cemetery?" she says. "That was the first place we ever went, remember?"

TJ tucks Alice into his coat as they walk all the way to Oakdale Cemetery. Many of the graves have Christmas plants on them, or pine boughs, and the place is magical and hushed in the snowfall. "Silent Snow, Secret Snow," Noli thinks. It is the title of a short story she read once for English class.

"Do you believe in immortality?" TJ asks her.

"Gee," she says softly, "I don't know. I mean . . . I would *like* there to be life after death, but who can say? Maybe a part of us endures. I don't know."

"A part of us does endure," TJ replies, "because I felt it when my grandmother died. I was very close to her, and when she died I kept feeling she was still there. She was all around me—as though her spirit hadn't left yet. As though she was still looking after me."

"How old were you?"

"Thirteen. I adored her."

It is the first thing about himself—the first personal thing—he has ever told her, and Noli is impressed. "What was she like?" she asks.

"Small, white-haired, beautiful. And totally accepting. I mean, she had complete acceptance of people just as they were. No prejudice, no criticisms. It helped me so much when I was little—because people were always on my back."

About what? Noli wants to ask, but doesn't. It is enough that he is sharing these things with her, these first confidences.

"What was her name, TJ?"

"Caroline Ross. She was a writer, like my dad. . . . God, she had such faith in me. She used to tell me I could be anything I wanted to be—anything in the world."

"No one's ever had faith in me that way," Noli says.

"Wrong," TJ replies. "I do."

In that moment, Noli longs to tell him that what she feels for him is greater than love, greater than anything personal. What she feels for him is connected to the universe and its mystery—sun, moon, and stars—but she cannot find the words. Then they both watch as an old woman walks up the path, approaches one of the graves, and kneels by it.

It is like a scene from a movie—with the snow falling and this anonymous old lady kneeling on the ground. She is dressed in a shabby coat, but she has two yellow roses with her, and carefully she places them on the grave. Her lips are moving with silent words.

Noli decides that the grave belongs to the woman's husband and she comes here every Christmas. And it's so sad, but also inspiring ... because maybe they were married a long time—like fifty years—and maybe they loved each other to the end. That is how she will love TJ, she thinks. To the very end. To the time when one of them comes here and lays two yellow roses on a grave.

11

Noli and TJ have decided to go into New York on New Year's Day—to see the tree at Rockefeller Center and take in a film. Noli's mother has offered to babysit with Alice, and so they will have a whole day together. At nine in the morning they board the Jitney in Sag Harbor, and as the bus rolls towards the city they talk or read magazines. The Jitney is very elegant and Noli has only been on it a few times in her life. You get coffee and juices on this bus, and a free newspaper.

They are both dressed in stonewashed jeans, boots, heavy jackets, and wool caps—and TJ thinks they look like twins. Noli would have liked to wear something more feminine, but since TJ prefers them to dress alike, she complies. TJ got a hundred dollars for Christmas and intends to spend it all on this one occasion. They will go to a good restaurant and a film, and buy books. It is a shining day—with bright sun and a hard blue sky—and the two of them are happy.

The bus lets them off at Forty-ninth Street on the East Side, and they walk over to Rockefeller Center to look at the

Christmas tree. It is a fantastic sight—the tallest tree Noli has ever seen—and it glitters with a thousand lights. Beyond the tree, skaters are going around and around the ice rink. They are human butterflies, turning and swooping.

Noli and TJ have an expensive lunch in the restaurant that looks out at the rink. The skaters are so good they are like professionals, leaping, twirling, gliding over the rainbow ice. And suddenly Sag Harbor seems very small and far away.

TJ has bought a copy of *New York* magazine, and they search the movie listings. "Oh, wow," says Noli. "There's a Dietrich double feature down in Greenwich Village."

"I don't like the Village much," says TJ. "Too dangerous."

"But TJ, it's daytime—and one of the films is *The Blue Angel*. We've never seen it."

"What's the other one?"

"*The Garden of Allah*. With Dietrich and Charles Boyer."

"Well . . ."

"Oh, please! We've never seen either of them. We could take a cab."

The movie theater is on West Houston Street, and they go inside just as *The Blue Angel* is starting. TJ holds her hand all through it, but during the second film—the one with Boyer—he hunches down into himself. It is as though he has forgotten her, as though the film is absorbing him completely.

When they come out onto the street—into the soft blue twilight—they feel dreamy and remote. The film with Boyer was like some kind of fairy tale set in the desert, and it was beautiful. Their bus doesn't leave for Long Island until eight o'clock, so they decide to go somewhere for a sandwich. Just as they are heading for a place TJ knows on Greenwich Avenue, they are stopped by a very weird young man. Noli thinks he is going to panhandle them—hustle them—but instead he says to TJ, "My God, TJ. Is it you?"

TJ's face looks blank. This character is wearing rhinestone earrings and eye shadow, and his hair is bleached platinum blond. He has on men's clothes—but women's high heels.

"Sorry," says TJ. "I don't know you."

"But sweetie, you *do*," says the man. "We met at Vincent's birthday party a year ago. Have you heard anything from him lately? Vincent, I mean."

"I don't know you," TJ says coldly. He takes Noli's arm and starts off—but the young man follows them.

"There is no need to be *snotty*," he says. "I was only trying to say hello."

"Shove off," says TJ.

"My *God*, we're being high and mighty. But maybe you're already occupied tonight, darling. Who's the trick?"

And that's when TJ hauls off and punches him—right in the middle of the street. Noli is so shocked she cannot move.

The young man staggers to his feet and looks at TJ. "You little shit!" he screams. "I'm going to call the police."

"Go to hell," TJ says—and then he and Noli start to run.

They run all the way across Greenwich Avenue and into a hamburger joint. TJ's face is pale, and Noli is terrified. She doesn't know what has happened, or why it happened. None of it makes sense.

They choose a table and order cups of coffee. And Noli sees that TJ is shaking. She puts her hand on his arm. "It's OK," she says, "it's over now. But what was it all about?"

"I don't know," TJ mumbles.

"Why did he think he knew you?"

"I don't know, I . . . maybe I met him once. My parents and I used to live down here, on Twelfth Street."

"He called you TJ. Like he knew you."

"I *told* you, I do not know him! He's a drag queen, a freak."

"Right," says Noli. After a second, she says softly, "He thought I was a guy."

"I know."

"He thought I was a young guy. God! I really must grow my hair longer, TJ. And wear dresses."

"Forget it. You're fine."

They have sandwiches and coffee in silence. Then TJ says, "Look Noli, my father's a writer and he meets all kinds of people. Artists, actors . . . I might have met that guy at a party or something. With my dad."

"Sure."

"Which is why I didn't want to bring you down here. The whole Village is filled with freaks."

An hour later they are on the Jitney, leaving the city. The sky has turned the color of ink, and as the bus heads east the large apartment buildings in Queens glitter with lights. Then the buildings disappear, and soon there are no lights at all—only a darkness that slips by to the rhythmic sound of the engine, the smooth thudding of the tires.

TJ has been holding Noli's hand. But now he gives a sigh and puts his head on her shoulder. Soon he is asleep, like a child who has had a long day, and as she gazes at his vulnerable face, she feels her heart tighten. She is so glad—and so relieved—to be heading home.

12

The next weeks are filled with school, too much homework, and conferences with guidance counselors about college. TJ has decided he wants to go to Bennington, in Vermont—which is almost impossible for Noli to imagine—but she has not the slightest idea where she wants to go, or even if she is college material. Her grades are undistinguished, and the only thing that really interests her at the moment is training Alice. She has taken books out of the library on how to housebreak a puppy, leash-train a puppy, and do puppy obedience work—and it is absorbing her completely. "Maybe I should become a dog trainer," she says to TJ. "Or run a pet store or something." TJ starts to laugh. It is obvious he cannot see her running a pet store.

The subject of college is causing a good deal of discussion at home too. Noli's mother insists she go to college, while her father is not so sure. "Look," Noli overhears him saying one night to her mother, "she'll probably get married young, like we did. So what's the point of college? Do you know what colleges cost these days? Twenty thousand a year. Thirty thousand. It's crazy."

They are standing in the kitchen having this discussion, while Noli eavesdrops from the dining room. "If I had gone to college my whole life would have been different," her mother says.

"Oh, Sally . . ."

"Well, it would have! Without an education a woman can't get a decent job."

"She won't need a job if she marries well."

"What do you want her to do? Marry that TJ?"

"She could do worse," says Noli's father. "They have a lot of money."

Her mother's voice drops, and Noli has to strain to hear her words. "I would *never* let her marry that boy, Harold. I've said that to you before."

"I thought you were crazy about him! You're all over him when he comes to visit."

"I try to like him for Noli's sake, but deep down I don't. There's something . . . strange about him. I can't put it into words."

"Come on, now. He's just sensitive. Artistic."

"It's not that—it's something deeper. It frightens me."

At that point, her mother had closed the kitchen door and Noli had gone up to her room. But the conversation had shocked her—the part about TJ.

The winter days come to a close by four in the afternoon, and the skies are gray for weeks at a time. Noli and TJ take walks along the deserted Wharf, or go to Oakdale Cemetery. They never see the old woman in the shabby coat again, and the two yellow roses have blown away.

On the surface, things are good between them. They roam the secondhand bookstores, looking for books on film, and every Saturday night they go to the Sag Harbor movie house for a double feature. It seems as though things are fine, but Noli knows differently. Something in the relationship has changed them into pals, buddies, whereas they should have become lovers.

This is causing Noli a great deal of pain, but she doesn't know what to do about it. TJ still kisses her, and they hold hands in the movies and take walks with their arms around each other—but there is something impersonal about it. Every kid in the school thinks they are making out—even Tracy—and girls cast sidelong glances at Noli in the hallways. They envy her for having sex with TJ Baker. But none of it is true.

There are doubts inside her now—doubts she never had before—and they make her feel a little sick, as though she has contracted a subtle illness. The doubts make her feel that she and TJ have been unreal to each other and that their closeness is an act. Maybe if she is patient things will change for them, but she knows that something is very wrong. There is either something wrong with TJ, or her, or both of them.

She is still having that terrible dream—the one about being lost in the city, lost in a maze of buildings and no way of getting home. Alice has entered the dream now, and sometimes Noli is searching the entire city for Alice, knowing the puppy is hungry and cold, knowing she must find her and bring her back to Sag Harbor. . . . One night she wakes from this dream with tears coming down her face. "I want to go home!" she cries into the darkness.

During the day she thinks about the dream. She has a physical home, with her parents and Alice, and Peterson High is also a kind of home, so what does the dream mean? She looks up the word "home" in an unabridged dictionary, and is surprised to learn that one of the meanings of the word is "one's abode after death."

Finally she decides that home means safety—and she has none. Safety would be TJ's arms around her. Safety would be her and TJ in a warm bed, learning to make love.

She has stopped shoplifting, which was a crazy habit to begin with, because she neither liked nor needed all the stuff she stole. From the dime store, mostly. And she is trying very hard to drink less—or at least not to drink around TJ. But the vodka is such a comfort she cannot kick the habit. She is tense a good deal of the time, and alcohol eases the tension. She likes the way it feels going down her throat into her belly. Warm and all-pervading, like an embrace.

Without alcohol she wouldn't have smuggled Alice into school that day in February. But she had taken a shot of vodka in the morning—mixed with orange juice—and suddenly it seemed like a good idea to take Alice to school and smuggle her through the system. Well, she tried this—and was able to keep Alice hidden in her jacket for two classes. But in Spanish III Alice escaped, ran up to Mrs. Nordio's desk, squatted, and peed. Everyone thought this was hilarious except Mrs. Nordio, who ordered Noli to take Alice home, and then said she was putting Noli on report.

During the first week of March something unusual happens. Noli's parents decide to go to Montreal for the weekend, to visit friends. Which means that Noli and TJ will have the house to themselves for two days. This opportunity obsesses Noli and she can think of nothing else. She has never seduced anyone—and wouldn't know how if she tried—but something tells her if she and TJ don't become lovers now, they never will.

Noli's parents leave for the airport on a Friday afternoon, and she invites TJ for dinner that night. He is aware of the two days stretching before them, and he seems nervous about it. Noli is not a great cook, but she prepares a chicken dinner with mashed potatoes and gravy. She shampoos her hair—which is below her ears now—and puts on a clean pair of jeans and a turtleneck sweater. Just before TJ arrives, she drinks a small glass of vodka—rinsing her mouth out afterwards with Listerine.

TJ comes to the door with six red roses. It is the first time he has ever brought her flowers, and she is thrilled. They kiss shyly and stand looking at each other. "Alone at last," he says, and gives a little laugh.

"Not quite alone," says Noli. "We have Alice."

TJ puts his arms around her. "You look beautiful," he says.

13

In the weeks to come, Noli will look back on this evening with a combination of feelings—rage, grief, confusion, despair. She will never be able to think of the incident without pain, and it seems like it will be this way forever. Maybe someday, when she is old, the memory of this evening will have softened. But not for a long time.

The dinner goes well enough, with TJ praising her cooking and taking second helpings of everything. They scrape the dishes, put them in the dishwasher, and take Alice out for a walk. They come back to the house and turn on the TV—switching channels until they find an old film, *That Hamilton Woman,* with Laurence Olivier. They sit on the living room couch and hold hands, watching the movie. It is ten o'clock and the neighborhood is quiet.

"I think I'll have a drink," TJ says abruptly. "What have you got in the house?"

Noli stares at him. "But you never drink, TJ."

"Well, tonight I feel like one. And anyway, *you've* been

drinking—I can smell it on your breath—so I might as well too."

Noli goes to the kitchen and pours them each a glass of vodka, with ice cubes and wedges of lemon. She brings the drinks back to the living room and TJ takes a large gulp of his, grimacing as it goes down. "God, that's strong. What is it?"

"Polish vodka. It's very expensive."

"Make me another," he says.

They both have a second drink, and TJ turns off some lights and builds a fire in the fireplace. He does this expertly, and at the touch of a match the fire blooms like a rose—opening and expanding in pink and yellow flames. He takes Noli's hand and pulls her down on the rug in front of the fire, and somehow the whole thing is a bit theatrical—like the movie they have been watching. And yet his arms are around her tightly for the first time, and he is kissing her deeply for the first time, and it seems like they are about to become lovers. The thing is . . . he is being rough about it. Without much delicacy he is pulling off her clothes—first her jeans and sweater, then her underwear.

He kisses her tiny breasts and she shudders at the feel of his mouth. Then he takes off his clothes and lies naked beside her.

Noli is stunned by the beauty of his body, and she is afraid of nothing now, and all the old worries about sex have disappeared. His body is golden by the fire, and the light catches chestnut colors in his hair and softens the coldness in his eyes . . . but he is not sexually aroused.

"I love you," she whispers. "I'll love you all my life." There are no responding words from him. He has gone very quiet, as the fire burns lower and a spatter of rain hits the window.

They lie in each other's arms for a long time, not kissing, not moving, as the fire turns into glowing coals and a winter storm begins—a storm made up of rain and wet snow. Alice pads into the room and lies down against Noli's bare legs. The room is so quiet that Noli can hear the beating of her own heart.

At last she says the words that must be said—and her voice breaks a little as she says them. "You're gay aren't you?" she says to TJ.

He begins to sob, weeping like a little boy, and the sobbing is her answer. And how strange it is—that she has known this for such a long time, but never made it conscious. The thought was buried in her mind like a dark jewel.

"It's OK," she says. "I understand—really. Just talk to me."

It is moments before he can speak, and then he does so in the midst of tears. "I'm sorry . . . you have to forgive me."

"I do. Really."

He reaches for his clothes and pulls them on, so she does the same. They sit on the rug facing each other. "Don't hate me," he says to her. "Please. I couldn't bear that."

"I don't hate you, TJ. I love you better than anything in the world."

"Try to understand . . ."

"I will."

"It's not that I don't love you. It's just that, well, I've

always been this way. I thought I could change. I mean, Jesus, I wanted to change *so much*."

"But you can't?"

"I was born this way. I'm homosexual. I can't help it."

"Do your parents know?"

"Yes. They had me in therapy for a whole year. It really hurts them."

"Therapy didn't help?"

"No! I just told you—I was born this way."

"Have you . . . had a lot of experience?" she asks.

He nods, his face turned away from her. "For a long time now I've been picking up guys and going home with them. Older guys, mostly. I've had a lot of sex with older guys."

She is too stunned to speak, but finally she says, "Go on."

"It started out with me just going to gay bars and dancing with people. I really like to dance that way. But pretty soon I was going home with them."

"What about AIDS?" she says dully. "Did that ever occur to you?"

"Of course it occurred to me! I'm not stupid. I use condoms."

"What kind of sex did you have with these men?"

"I don't want to go into that."

"Why not?" she says tensely. "We're being honest, aren't we?"

"Noli, look . . ."

"What do you do with these people?"

"That's none of your business. I'm sorry."

And that's when she explodes—all of her goodwill disappearing. "Well, I think it *is* my business! Why did you and your parents move here in the first place? Because you got into trouble in the Village?"

"Well, yes, but . . ."

"And who was I supposed to be? Your new cure?"

"It isn't like that!"

"Who am I supposed to be? An experiment that will turn you straight? God! What a coward you are."

"Noli . . ."

"No wonder we never made out! It probably sickened you to touch me."

"That's not it at all."

"You chose me because I look like a boy!"

"Not true. I love you."

"Do not use that word to me!" she screams. "You dirty faggot."

TJ rises to his feet. "I'm going home now. I've had it with you."

"And I have had it with *you!*" she yells. "You rotten queer. If you ever speak to me again I'll have you arrested! Go back to what you were before. Fuck men. Hundreds of men. But leave me alone!"

TJ gathers himself up to his full height and looks her square in the eye. "I love you, Noli," he says quietly. "You're the best thing in my life—and that's the truth."

The minute he is gone she goes into the kitchen and pours herself a drink. She brings it back to the living room, sits down on the rug, and gulps the vodka. Then she smashes the glass into the fireplace.

Alice, who has been frightened by all the commotion,

creeps back to Noli and gets on her lap. She wags her tail and licks Noli's face, as if to say, "I'm here, everything's OK."

"Oh, Alice," Noli says, burying her face in the dog's curly hair. "What have I done?"

14

Two days later Noli walks into English III, expecting to see TJ and dreading it. But TJ does not arrive. Mr. Cameron explains that TJ asked to be transferred to another English class because of a schedule conflict. So Noli does not see him that morning, and when she shows up for the film elective, he is not there either. It seems that within the space of one morning he has invented some fantastic story and rearranged his entire schedule, so he won't have to see her. She does not spot him at lunchtime, and by three o'clock he has vanished. Just as she is getting ready to go home, Tracy comes up to her and asks where TJ is. Is he sick or something? Tracy wants to know. "No," says Noli. "We broke up."

It was unwise to say this to Tracy—to say it before Noli can even decide if it's true—because by the next day the news has spread all over school. She hadn't realized Tracy would tell every single person at Peterson High that she and TJ are no longer a couple—but Tracy has done this out of spite, getting even for being neglected for six months. On

Tuesday, a girl Noli barely knows comes up to her and says, "God. I'm so sorry about you and TJ," which makes Noli furious. "Get lost," she says to the girl. "You don't know what you're talking about."

On Wednesday she cuts her hair so short it looks like a crew cut. And on Thursday she comes to school drunk. Immediately, she is put on report and a note sent home to her parents. She is also forced to take blood and urine tests—which is humiliating.

Noli's parents are asked to come to school to discuss the incident with the school psychologist. The psychologist sees Noli privately and talks about AA. There is a teenage group that meets on Friday nights, the psychologist says. "Forget it," Noli replies, and walks out of the room.

She is in trouble everywhere—with her parents, with the school—but mostly in trouble with herself. She is drunk every day, which is a shock to her mother, who never knew she drank at all, but Noli refuses to discuss it. "None of your business," she says to Sally Brown—and is promptly locked in her room. Her father tries to reason with her, kindly, calmly, but Noli will not listen. Then her parents realize TJ is no longer coming around, and they try to talk about that, but Noli has lost control—like some crazy car on the highway. They stop her allowance, and she steals from her mother's purse. They discover this, and she hocks her CD player—in order to buy booze.

TJ's absence in her life is so painful she feels she will die of it. She does not know how to function without him, because there is no one to talk to now, no one to hug, and no one to walk her home—whistling that sad little tune.

There is no one to go to the cemetery with, so Noli goes alone and sits on a bench near the grave where the old woman placed the roses. She takes Alice with her sometimes, and sits there with the dog on her lap in the March weather, the changeable weather that sweeps through the town with snow and rain and the high honking of geese. Geese are passing over the town in great numbers, always in the shape of a V, and their cries are so forlorn they tear Noli's heart. She wishes she could fly with them, over the winter town, towards a sudden paradise where she will never know pain again.

15

She does of course see TJ during the next weeks, because it would be impossible not to. She sees him hurrying from one class to another, or out on the hockey field playing like a demon. She sees him coming out of Luckey's Market with a bottle of Coke—and every time she sees him her heart contracts with sorrow. But she will not give in. He has duped her, and his entire position these past six months has been a fraud. All that talk about God, and poetry, and no drugs, and vegetarian food. . . .

Noli thinks of all the times TJ said "I love you" to her, and feels sick inside. She remembers his head on her shoulder as they came back from the city that night—and she realizes he *did* know the weird guy who wore women's high heels, and God knows who else. He was probably making out the whole time he dated her.

Noli tries to imagine the sex acts TJ does with men. She tries to visualize the details, but cannot. It seems so awful. But she has read somewhere that gay men like anonymous sex, so maybe that is what gives TJ pleasure—a lack of involvement. She herself was too involved, of course. She was like a puppy trotting after him, a sycophant, a slave.

Exactly one week after she and TJ have parted, Noli finds a letter shoved under the door of her school locker. It is sealed tightly with Scotch tape.

Noli: Please don't hate me. I see you marching around school and you seem filled with hate. What you don't understand is that I really do love you. It may not be a sexual love, but it's real and true . . . You were right about me getting in trouble in the city. I was arrested. I know that sounds terrible, but I'm different now. I'm trying so hard to purify my life, trying so hard to find out who I am. I wasn't using you, Noli. I loved and honored you. And I still do.

TJ

She tears up the letter and throws it away. And once again, she gets drunk. But the school psychologist has told her she will be suspended if she doesn't go to the Friday night AA group, so—in a fury—she goes. It is held in a church basement on Madison Street and consists of ten teenagers sitting around a table, talking about their drinking. The person leading the group is also a teenager— no adults present—and at the back of the room is a table with refreshments. Coffee, cookies, soft drinks. Noli is amazed that before anyone speaks he or she says, "My name is John and I'm an alcoholic," or "My name is Melissa and I'm an alcoholic." When it comes her turn to speak, Noli refuses to say this. Instead, she says, "I'm here because they're going to suspend me from school if I don't come. But I don't want to be here, and I don't think I'm an alcoholic." People laugh at this, but not in a cruel way. They laugh as though they have heard it before.

"I'm not kidding you," Noli says to the group. "I've been drunk a few times in my life, but I'm not an alcoholic."

"What do you think an alcoholic *is?*" a boy named Tommy asks her.

"Well . . ." Noli begins. But she doesn't know how to continue.

"If drinking interferes with your life in any way, you're an alcoholic," says a girl.

"Right," says Tommy. "Like, has it interfered with your schoolwork, or your life at home? Has anyone complained about it to you?"

Noli thinks of all of TJ's complaints. "No one's ever complained," she lies.

But on the way home she does some thinking about it. The kids in the group—two of whom are from Peterson High—are totally honest in the way they talk about themselves. Some of them have horrendous stories to tell—about drinking and driving, getting arrested, winding up in jail—and yet they don't seem reluctant to admit these things. Noli finds the whole thing interesting, but not for her. And when she gets home she goes straight to her room, takes a hidden bottle of vodka out of the closet, and has a drink.

A few days later she has a confrontation with Tracy. It was bound to happen—because they are practically enemies now—but the meeting disturbs Noli because it is so unexpected. She is just about to leave school at three o'clock, when Tracy confronts her in their homeroom. "I need to talk to you," Tracy says coldly. "That is, if you've got a minute."

"What's on your mind?" Noli says.

"People say you're going to be suspended, so I wanted to ask you in person. Is it true?"

"Would you care if it was true?"

Tracy shrugs. "Yes and no. I mean, you and I haven't been close for a long time . . . but I did want to know."

"I'm not going to be suspended, OK? Everything's under control."

"Have you seen TJ since the two of you broke up?"

"I don't want to talk about it, Tracy."

"The only reason I'm asking is, well, I guess you know he's got a new friend. I mean, everybody knows that."

Noli's heart sinks like an elevator. "No," she says casually, "I didn't know. What's her name?"

"It's not a her, it's a *him*. His name is Walker Lewis and he goes to that new prep school in East Hampton."

"The Windward School?"

"Right. Windward. They're together all the time now, TJ and Walker. Real buddies."

Noli realizes that Tracy is not implying anything. She hasn't the slightest idea TJ is gay, and neither has anyone else. TJ has made a new start in The Hamptons—after being arrested for prostitution, or whatever it was—but now there is this new person in his life. Walker.

"I'm not really interested in what TJ does," Noli says. "It's ancient history. OK?"

"Sure," Tracy replies. "I just wondered if you knew."

They stand there looking at each other with a mixture of feelings—resentment, jealousy, affection—and it is very painful. Tracy looks beautiful, with her long hair cascading about her shoulders and just a hint of makeup on her perfect face. Unlike Noli, she is obsessed with clothes and is wearing some very chic pants with a loose black pullover. Noli's clothes are a wreck.

"Well, I've got to go now," Tracy says. "Be seeing you."

"Sure," Noli replies, "see you around." But on the way home she feels lost. She and Tracy were so close once, and now they are strangers. As for TJ . . . it is amazing he has found a new person so soon.

During the next few weeks Noli begins to do something she is ashamed of. It isn't shoplifting, and it certainly isn't drugs. What she has begun doing is spying on TJ. She wants to see him with Walker Lewis so she will understand the nature of their relationship. It is possible TJ and Walker are just friends, but somehow she doubts it. Her instinct tells her Walker has replaced her, and that TJ chose him on the rebound. People who are on the rebound, Noli thinks, often get involved with new people very quickly—as a way of easing their sadness—and sometimes the new people are inappropriate. This Walker Lewis could be *anyone*—a hood, a degenerate, a pothead. And it means nothing that he goes to a fancy prep school. Kids like that are often the worst.

She begins following TJ after school—and pretty soon her spying pays off. On a Thursday, outside of Luckey's Market, TJ and a tall blond kid are sitting on a bench drinking seltzer. The blond kid has hair as long as TJ's and he is startlingly handsome. Not just good-looking, but gorgeous. The two of them are like Greek gods, and they are laughing and talking as though they have known each other forever.

Noli stands at a distance and watches them—and it's odd, but the thing that hurts her the most is that TJ and Walker are both wearing baseball caps, put on backwards. And they are wearing dirty white Levi's and baggy sweaters. So it is obvious that TJ has a new twin.

She is standing across the street, shielded by a big oak tree, and she knows they cannot see her. Walker takes out some cigarette paper and rolls a cigarette. The sun gets in his eyes and he tosses his head impatiently. Noli cannot see his eyes, but she knows they are ice blue, and cold, like TJ's. And she also knows that Walker and TJ are lovers. Nobody else would think of this, because the boys are so macho, but she knows that when they are alone they have secrets nobody else can share. Secrets of the body and the mind, secrets that bring them pleasure. She knows they have been naked together, and given sex to each other, and fallen asleep afterwards like tired children. And what is *she* now but a kind of voyeur—an outsider destined to watch and dream.

16

Throughout the month of April, Noli spies on TJ and his new friend. She follows them through the streets of Sag Harbor and once even goes into The Purple Grape, where they are eating dinner. They are at a table in the corner and do not see her, so she buys some yogurt and leaves—feeling ashamed of herself. But no matter how ashamed she feels, she cannot stop following them. Walker's school obviously lets out earlier than Peterson High, because he shows up every day at three o'clock in the parking lot of Peterson, waiting for TJ. Walker has a Honda motorcycle—not just a little motorbike, but a big machine with all sorts of compartments for carrying things, and a wide saddle on the back. To see them take off on this machine is like seeing something out of a Batman movie, both boys wearing helmets and goggles and leaning into the wind.

It is not "anonymous sex" Noli realizes, because the boys seem almost married to each other, and the few times she is able to watch them up close they seem deeply connected.

How fantastic that nobody knows they are gay! But hell, she thinks, Walker is as good an athlete as TJ, and people at Peterson say he is really something at the beach. He has learned to surf in Hawaii, on vacations with his parents, and teaches surfing to some of the younger kids. He is also brilliant at basketball.

Noli is overwhelmed with regret. Regret over the terrible things she said to TJ, and the fact that she was not compassionate when he unburdened himself. Another kind of girl would have been compassionate. But she, with her quick temper, simply flew off the handle.

Oh God, she says to herself, if I had just been understanding with him he'd still be with me. If I'd simply *accepted* him he'd still be here—holding my hand, kissing my cheek, walking me home. How could I have been so stupid and selfish, so mean. . . . She thinks of all the nice things he did for her—giving her Alice, bringing her the roses—and feels sick with regret, and longing.

She goes to the local library and takes out some books on homosexuality. They all have different theories about the subject, but at least three of the books say homosexuality isn't a choice. People are born that way, say the books, and there's nothing they can do about it. When TJ had said this she hadn't believed him—but now she is beginning to wonder. Maybe TJ had no more choice in the matter than *she* did when she was born straight . . . and one of the books even suggests that gayness is simply the flip side of straightness. In other words, the two behaviors are very much alike except for the sex of the partner. This thought amazes Noli, and she dwells on it for days.

On Easter morning, she puts Alice's collar and leash on and prepares to go out for a walk. As she closes the front door, she sees a vase of flowers on the steps, and the card with the flowers says "Noli." She opens the card and feels all of her pain beginning again—because the flowers are from TJ.

Dear Noli: These flowers are to wish you a Happy Easter and to tell you that I still love you. I wish we could be friends because I miss you so badly. I know you must know about Walker by now, but that is something different—not connected to us at all. He's good for me, Noli, because we're the same age and he's a stable kind of person. I even introduced him to my parents the other day—trying to be honest about everything. Noli, could you ever be friends with me? I miss you so.

TJ

The flowers are a mixture of tulips and daffodils, arranged in a green vase. But they only make her angry—so angry, in fact, that she takes the arrangement and leaves it on a neighbor's porch. "I don't want anything from you," she says aloud to TJ. "So you can take your Easter present and shove it."

But this is not really the truth. The truth is that she is confused by TJ's offer of friendship and doesn't know what to do about it. It fills her with ambivalence. Then she thinks of the words, "He's good for me, Noli, because we're the same age and he's a stable kind of person." How cruel it was to say that.

She walks Alice up to the cemetery, sits down on the stone bench where she and TJ used to sit, and takes out a flask of vodka. It is only eight in the morning, but she needs a drink, and carrying a flask amuses her. She found it in her dad's closet, in a box of old things he keeps—an antique silver flask from days gone by. "Happy Easter," she says to Alice, and takes a swallow of the silvery liquid.

The vodka burns going down, but then the familiar warmth comes into her belly and she relaxes. The day is brilliant and clear, with a pale blue sky and the smell of spring everywhere. There are clumps of daffodils growing around the graves, and birds are singing their spring songs, and a squirrel is sitting on a gravestone holding a nut in his paws. All these new beginnings, she says to herself, and for what? Everything dies in the end—birds, flowers, relationships—and there is nothing you can count on.

After a few more drinks, Noli decides it would be fun for Alice to run around off-leash. She has only been allowed to do this once, at the ocean beach, and she isn't very good about coming when called, but what the hell, let her have some fun. "Go chase squirrels," she says to Alice, removing the leash. "Have a good time."

Alice does exactly that—taking off after a squirrel, and then running in happy circles around the graves. She doesn't go very far, and after a while Noli forgets about her. She has had three drinks and they are affecting her, probably because she only had a doughnut for breakfast.

She closes her eyes and breathes in the odors of spring. Rain-soaked daffodils, new grass growing, and that lovely smell that comes from the ocean. The ocean is six miles away, but she can smell it here in the cemetery—a salt smell that is mixed with flowers and damp earth and wheat growing in the fields. The thing about The Hamptons is the combination of farmlands and the sea, Noli says to herself. That's why people come here every summer. Maybe I'll buy a farm one day and have all the animals I want. Dogs, cats, cows, even a donkey. . . .

She dreams on for a while, then opens her eyes and calls for Alice. But the puppy is nowhere to be seen. "Alice!" she calls more loudly, getting to her feet, but there is only silence.

She can't have gone far, Noli thinks, she never goes very far—but there is no trace of Alice, and suddenly such fear comes into Noli's heart that she is almost sober again. Alice doesn't have a tag on, or any kind of identification, because Noli took off her collar and leash to let her run around.

For the next two hours, Noli searches the cemetery and the adjoining neighborhood, calling for Alice. She calls until she is hoarse, but the puppy is gone.

By three that afternoon Alice has not appeared—and Noli's parents have called the police, the animal shelter, and have put a "missing dog" announcement on the local radio station. They have also put up signs around the neighborhood. Noli is in tears and is walking around the town pond calling for Alice when her father comes and finds her. "She'll turn up by tomorrow," he says gently to Noli. "You just wait and see."

17

But Alice does not turn up, and when Noli returns to school—after Easter vacation—she is pale and drawn. The loss of Alice has been her fault, hers alone, and she is so grief-stricken she has made a bargain with God. It is not one of her usual small bargains. It is a very big one. Dear God, she says silently, if you will just bring Alice back I'll stop drinking. I mean this. I will never touch liquor again.

She cannot bring herself to tell TJ about Alice, but she does tell her Friday-night AA group—and they are sympathetic. "We know how you feel," one of the girls says to Noli. "It's awful to lose a pet."

"She was only five months old," Noli says. "A puppy."

"She could still turn up," one of the boys says hopefully. "My dog did that after being gone for two months. I'm not kidding. He was lost for two months."

"The trouble is . . ." Noli says hesitantly, "the whole thing makes me want to drink more than ever."

"That's normal," says the boy, whose name is Chris.

"You don't have to wait to stop drinking until Alice

comes back," Noli's new friend Melissa says. "Stop drinking anyway."

And so Noli does. It is not an easy thing to do, but she stops. At first she feels sick, really sick, from withdrawal—and then life suddenly seems empty. Without alcohol to warm her she feels that her heart is frozen, her mind is frozen, and she has turned into a corpse. Alcohol was warmth and color and excitement and instant love—and now there is nothing to replace it, nothing but the Friday-night meetings, which Melissa says are enough. But they aren't enough—not yet—so Noli walks through the world like a living corpse.

Her grades at school have plummeted, and she looks like a street person most of the time—with holes in her sneakers and spiky hair that stands straight up—but she is sober, and has added two more AA meetings to her schedule. She now goes to adult meetings on Wednesday and Saturday, as well as the teenage group, and she is beginning to "get the program," as the old-timers say. There is a lot of pride connected with this—especially since her parents are so pleased with her sobriety—but it doesn't change the fact that Alice is gone. Both Alice and TJ came into her life and departed as swiftly as the birds who dart through the back garden. . . . The town is turning towards summer, with longer days and hot bright skies—and the first sailboats are coming into the harbor, their sails spread like wings. The tourist shops are opening again, and The Anchor, on the Wharf, is serving again—and soon the Wharf theater will open and the outdoor concerts will begin on Bay Street.

It is harder to park in Sag Harbor now—you have to go

in early for your groceries and mail—and soon everything will have come full circle. One day the hot crowded tourist summer will be over and it will be September 5—a year to the day when she met TJ. It will be September 5 and if she had a sense of humor, or irony—which she doesn't anymore—she would go up to Oakdale and lay a wreath there, in memory of their love. She still loves TJ, and will probably love him forever, but a part of her has gone numb, as though someone shot Novocain into it. This numbness comes from the constant sight of TJ and Walker, who are such a regular couple that people don't even talk about them anymore. They are taken for granted—two macho kids who ride like greased lightning down Route 114 on Walker's motorcycle. Who can be seen in The Purple Grape, having vegetarian pizza. Who will soon be spending most of their time at the beach, surfing, kidding around with the girls, lying on the hot sand with radios blaring and an open bag of potato chips and a couple of Cokes. And, wonder of wonders, nobody thinks they are gay.

People in "the program," as the members call AA, keep telling Noli if she will just hang in there things will get better. So she hangs in, and does not drink, and phones Melissa—who has become her sponsor—twice a day, confiding in this new friend and saying over and over how much she wants to drink. "If you take it a day at a time, you can stay sober," Melissa says. And so Noli takes it a day at a time. One—difficult—day at a time.

She has assumed that sobriety will turn her life into sunshine and roses, but of course it does no such thing. Melissa explains this by saying sobriety doesn't take your problems away—but it does give you back your life.

"The problem is that I *have* no life," Noli says to Melissa one day, when they are walking along the Wharf. "Booze made me feel that my life was full, but it's not. It's completely empty."

"Not true," Melissa says absently. She is looking at a flock of sea gulls that are circling the water—and her cheeks are very pink. She is a slim girl with short black hair and wonderful, creamy skin. Like Tracy, her clothes are chic— bought in the city.

They stop walking and sit down on a bench, watching the sea gulls, who circle and cry and then take off towards Shelter Island. "You know what I hate about AA?" Noli says to Melissa.

"No," Melissa replies. "But I'm sure you'll tell me."

"What I hate is that everyone in the program is so goddamn *cheerful*. What have they got to be cheerful about? They've had rotten lives."

Melissa gives her a little smile. "Maybe they're glad to be alive. Ever think of that?"

"The cheerfulness of the whole thing makes me want to puke."

"Doesn't matter, Noli. Just keep going to meetings. Take it a day at a time."

"And those slogans! 'A day at a time.' 'First things first.' 'Easy does it.' It's all so corny."

Melissa, who is a very calm person, simply shrugs. She is an A-student at a school in Bridgehampton, and she is studying music with the hope of becoming a concert pianist. Noli has heard her play, and she is brilliant.

"I can leave any time I want," Noli says to Melissa, hoping to get a rise out of her. "I'm not married to the program or anything. I can always leave."

"Absolutely," says Melissa.

Noli still has her recurring dream about being lost in the city, and both TJ and Alice are in the dream now. They are searching for her just as hard as she is searching for them, but somehow they never connect with her, and, as usual, no one in the entire city of New York will help her get home. She wakes from the dream one morning with a new realization—which is that she doesn't hate TJ anymore. He is obviously trying to find a new and honorable way of being a gay person, and this is his right.

She tries to picture becoming friends with TJ and Walker—and draws a blank. She tries to imagine the three of them doing things together, and doesn't see how it could work out. Because she would see them loving each other, and the love between them would almost kill her. But maybe it would be a positive thing to do. She feels frightened much of the time, and has had some anxiety attacks that made her heart pound like a drum. Maybe being around TJ and Walker would be a comfort. Oh God, she says to herself, I am still so confused.

18

On the first Sunday in May the telephone in the Browns' kitchen rings, and Noli picks it up. She has been sitting at the kitchen table reading a magazine and eating a sandwich—and sun is streaming through the windows. Her parents are at a luncheon for the local real estate brokers.

"Hello?" Noli says into the phone.

"Did you lose a dog a few weeks ago?" a male voice says. "Is this the right number for the dog?"

Noli's heart goes very still, and for a moment she cannot reply. After a second she says, "Yes, it's the right number. We lost a black poodle on Easter Sunday."

"Well, I'll be darned!" says the man. "The reason I'm calling is, I saw one of your posters yesterday on a telephone pole, and I thought it might be the same dog. A small black poodle, right? Still sort of a puppy?"

"Yes!" Noli cries. "Did you find her? Is she OK? Is she alive?"

"Slow down, slow down," says the man. "We've got her and she's fine. What happened was this. We found her near the Whaler's Church on Easter Day, but we were just leaving for vacation—to Florida—so we took her with us. She didn't have a collar on or anything, so my wife figured she was a stray. We drove her to Florida with us, and we came back two days ago. What do you call her?"

"Alice," says Noli.

"*We* call her Curly. But it doesn't matter. Do you want her back? Your poster said there was a reward."

"There's a hundred-dollar reward," Noli says in a choked voice. "Where do you live? I'll come right now."

"The white house at the end of Glover Street. Number ten."

At first, Alice is not particularly excited to see Noli—but after a few minutes she warms up and is in Noli's arms, licking her face. She seems fine and healthy, though she does need a bath. "I think she's kind of mad at you," says the man, whose name turns out to be Mr. Foster. "Like you abandoned her."

Noli gives the Fosters a check for a hundred dollars and carries Alice home in her arms. "You've been to Florida," she says in an awed voice. "All the goddamn way to Florida. And I never knew it."

The first thing Noli does when they arrive home is fill the downstairs bathtub and immerse Alice in it. With fierce determination, she scrubs her with Vidal Sassoon shampoo—and dries her outdoors with a beach towel. At that point her parents come home, and her mother is so surprised to see Alice she bursts into tears.

In the years to come, Noli will always remember the moment when her mother cried. She never dreamed her mother cared so much about Alice—because she had put Alice the First to sleep at the vet's. But her love for Alice the Second was so real that day that a lump came into Noli's throat. Her mother had embraced the puppy, saying, "Oh Alice, you're home." And at that sudden moment the word "amends" came into Noli's mind. People in AA were always talking about amends, and now she understood what the word meant. She needed to make amends to her mother for all the cruel things she had said to her in the past. Because Sally Brown was just another suffering human being. Not a witch and not a monster. Just another suffering human being.

"You see?" Noli's father had said, while Sally hugged the dog. "I told you she'd come back. Noli sweetheart, you need more faith."

It's true, she thinks. She needs more faith in everything— in her parents, and AA, and the fact that someday she will find another boy to love. Melissa says so, and Melissa is the smartest kid Noli has ever met. The word "cool" might have been invented for her, she is so laid-back.

More than anything in the world, Noli would like to pick up the phone, call TJ, and tell him the story of Alice. She would like to say, "She went all the way to Florida, can you *believe* it?" but she still feels so alienated from TJ and Walker that she is paralyzed.

The love she feels for TJ Baker goes on and on. It is as though she became mixed with him and cannot free herself of his colors and his words. If she sees something beautiful, she sees it through his eyes. And when she hears good music, it is as though he is hearing it too. They never made love, and yet she feels he has entered her body and her mind. And how weird that romantic love is the thing most people long for, when romantic love can bring such pain. Everyone she has ever met wants to love another person, not realizing that the loss of the person can kill you because it reaffirms your loneliness—that basic loneliness everyone has when they come into the world, and when they leave it.

I wish I were brave enough to go through life by myself, Noli thinks. I wish I were brave enough to become a nun, an old maid, a crazy recluse. I wish I had the guts to live in the desert, or in a shack by the sea, and be totally self-sufficient. Just me and Alice.

19

Early in June, Noli sits down at her desk and writes her mother a letter. She is not sure if she will ever give her this letter—but there are things she wants to say. It has a lot to do with the word "amends."

Dear Mom,
There are twelve "steps" in AA, and one of these steps
has to do with making amends. I haven't reached that
step yet, but there are still things I want to say to you.
The first one is that I'm glad we're not fighting anymore.
It is like a huge weight off my heart. I hated fighting
with you, and often, though you didn't know it, I would
cry afterwards. Many of these fights were my fault
entirely—and I apologize.

I know you would have liked to have a more feminine
daughter—someone who was interested in clothes and
makeup and hair styles. But I'm not like that, and maybe
for the rest of my life I'll be what TJ once called a gamin.

I'm sorry if that hurts you, but it's just the way I am. . . .
I haven't been able to talk to you and Daddy about TJ,
and why we broke up, but someday I will.

You and I have never once said "I love you" to each
other, but I do love you, and I care about your life—
just as you care about mine.

I hope I have the courage to give you this letter, Mom.

> *fondly,*
> *Noli*

20

And now we return to the beginning of this story—with Noli standing in the doorway of a barber shop in early August. TJ has passed her on the street, wearing blue jeans, boots, and a white T-shirt—and his face is the face of an angel in a painting. He has a tan, from surfing all summer off the beach at Bridgehampton, and his curly brown hair is falling to his shoulders. A few steps behind him, his friend Walker is rolling a cigarette. He is tan too, from a summer at the beach, and his blond hair is almost white from the sun.

They look beautiful together. Not just handsome, but beautiful, two boys in torn blue jeans who have secrets between them she will never share. Their stride is identical, they are the same height, and it has been a long time since Noli first realized they were lovers. But these months have not been lost ones. She has sobered up and become very close to Melissa, and she is getting along well with her mother. She has enrolled in an obedience class with Alice, and has met a boy there named Terry who has actually invited her out. She didn't accept his invitations, but found them interesting—because she still looks like a zombie, with chopped-off red hair. What Terry sees in her she cannot imagine, but he has asked her for a date twice, and pretty soon she will accept. Terry has a blond crew cut and is not handsome, but very appealing, with a funny little smile and a gruff voice. He has an English bulldog named Winston, and he is catching on to the obedience work much faster than she is. "Bring Alice over to my house," he has said to Noli, "and we can practice the lessons together. Then we could go to a movie or something."

So the months and weeks have not been totally lost, and Noli is sober, but the sight of TJ and Walker passing on the street brings her to tears. She cries onto the back of her left hand as the boys stroll by, and—all over again—she wonders if she will ever be free of this love which has become a wound inside her. She carries her love like a battle scar, or one leg that is shorter than the other, and there is no pleasure in it anymore.

TJ and Walker are at least a block away, so she steps onto the sidewalk feeling safe. But then, to her horror, she sees TJ turning back. He has seen her and wants to say something. For a moment she panics—where can I run? she thinks—but it seems childish to run away, especially from someone who used to be her soul mate. "Noli!" TJ calls. "Wait up."

And then he is standing in front of her, looking more beautiful, and vulnerable, than ever—and he is so obviously glad to see her that it tears her apart. For months they have been avoiding each other, and now here he is, only a few inches away, smiling down at her with his sweet smile and gazing at her with eyes that are still ice blue, but no longer cold. His eyes are tinged with violet now. They are warm with summer and the sun. "Noli," he says tentatively.

She does something awkward—which is to stick out her hand. Looking embarrassed, he takes her hand and shakes it. "Noli," he says. "I'm so glad to see you."

For a moment, she can't think of anything to say. Finally, she says, "We've seen each other all spring. In school."

"I know, but . . . you always avoid me. I can't get near you."

"I thought it was you who was avoiding *me*," she says coldly.

"Not true! I've missed you terribly. Didn't you get my Easter present?"

"I got it. Thank you."

"Is Alice OK?"

Noli decides not to mention Alice's disappearance. "She's fine. I'm taking her to obedience class."

"That's great."

"We're the worst in the class. The instructor said so."

"I don't believe it, Noli. You're wonderful at anything you do."

He is looking at her with such longing that it confuses her. Then she sees tears in his eyes—and all of a sudden she doesn't know how to behave. Walker is standing at a distance, watching them.

"How have you been, TJ?" she asks.

"Pretty good. Fair."

"You *look* good. With that tan and everything."

"I've been going to the beach."

"With your friend?"

"Yes. With Walker."

"Are you happy?" she says. "With this new person?"

"Yes, but . . ."

"But what?"

"But I miss you! It's like losing a foot or something."

She smiles. "I've never been compared to a foot."

"I mean it, Noli. I miss you every minute."

"I miss you too."

"Those things you said to me . . . they really hurt."

"I know it, TJ, and I'm sorry. I apologize."

"Jesus!" he explodes. "Can't we be *friends*? Do we have to throw the whole thing away?"

No, she wants to reply, we cannot be friends. Melissa is my friend and someday Tracy will be my friend again, but you and I are not friends. We were soul mates once, and almost lovers, and therefore I cannot switch gears and become friends. I know you would like me to meet Walker—and go out with the two of you—and become the female buddy of two gay boys, but I cannot do this because I still love your body and your mind and the way your eyes are violet now. Soft and violet-colored from the sun.

Aloud, she says, "We were never friends, TJ. So why now?"

"God," he says, "if *we* weren't friends, who was?"

"Abbott and Costello. Martin and Lewis."

"Don't make fun of me, Noli. I still love you."

"As a friend?"

"Well, sure. But that doesn't mean the love isn't real."

Noli sighs. "TJ, we're not on the same wavelength. I

didn't love you as a friend. I wanted to be your lover, your mate . . . something like that."

"Love is love."

"No, it's not. There are different kinds of love, and the kind I felt for you was passionate. You didn't feel that way about me, that's all. I was a buddy."

"I don't distinguish between these things! If I love someone, I love them forever."

"So love me forever," she says tiredly, "and keep me in your mind like a beautiful dream—while you sleep with Walker."

"Noli, that's just so different."

"You bet it is."

TJ gazes at her. "Why are you being so tough?"

"Because I *am* tough," she replies. "These past months have made me tougher than you'd believe. I stopped drinking, did you know that? Well, actually you didn't because we haven't been in touch. But if we *had* been in touch you would have learned that I bit the bullet and joined AA. Talk about withdrawal! It was really hard. But I did it and I'm proud of myself—and I'm sorry, TJ Baker, but I cannot be your friend."

His eyes are filled with tears, and she wants to put her arms around him—but she doesn't. Something tells her that unless she breaks off with him now he will always be her prison, a beautiful box in which she is trapped. Her instinct tells her she needs to be free of him so she can find herself.

Yes, she says silently, that's it. I need to be free of you so I can find *me*. It isn't that we won't talk to each other in school next year—and maybe when you go off to college we'll write letters. And maybe the day will come when I'll have coffee with you and Walker at The Purple Grape, and go to a movie with you or something. All those things are possible. But not now, TJ. Not now.

"How have your parents been about Walker?" she asks him.

"Great," he replies. "Amazing. Mostly . . . they just want me to be happy."

"That's very enlightened."

"I know. They've come a long way."

"Listen, I have to go now," she says. "But I wish you well. I think you know that."

"I wish you well too," he says. "But it's hard without you."

She shrugs. "Everything's hard."

"How do you mean?"

She looks into his eyes—those blue eyes that are tinged with violet—and says, "Everything's hard, TJ. Life, death, loneliness. Getting sober when you don't want to. Making new friends. It's all very very hard. But we do it, don't we? Somehow we do it."

She turns on her heel and walks away. Then she looks back and gives TJ and Walker a brief, impersonal wave. She is not, after all, their enemy. And she doesn't want them to think she is.

21

That night Noli has the dream again. She is lost in a city of seven million people and she doesn't know how to get home. TJ isn't in the dream this time and neither is Alice—it is just her and the city, and the faceless seven million, none of whom will help her. She asks a taxi driver for help, and then a lady wheeling a baby carriage, but no one will listen. Home is at least three hours away, far down on Long Island, and because she has lost her wallet she cannot afford bus fare. She has lost her wallet and her house keys and cannot even remember her phone number. If she could just remember the number, she could call her parents and ask them to come and get her. But there is no one to help her—not her parents, or TJ, or Alice—and for a moment, within the dream, she thinks she will die of fear. She is not sure if a person can die of fear, but it seems possible.

"Please," she says within the dark waters of the dream. "Somebody help me! I need to go home."

Then—suddenly—the dream changes and Noli is on her way home. She can hardly believe this, but for the very first time the dream is allowing her to get back to Sag Harbor. She is on a large super-modern bus, and the bus is zooming along the expressway, cleaving the wind like the geese do when they fly in formation. She is on the most super-modern bus in the world, a bus that says "Sag Harbor" across the front of it, and an incredible feeling is coming into her. A feeling of joy. Everything looks so familiar! Golf courses, ponds, shopping centers. She has seen these places before—gone to these movie houses, eaten in these restaurants—and as the towns speed by her window, she knows that for the first time in her life she is coming home. She— Noli Brown—is coming home.